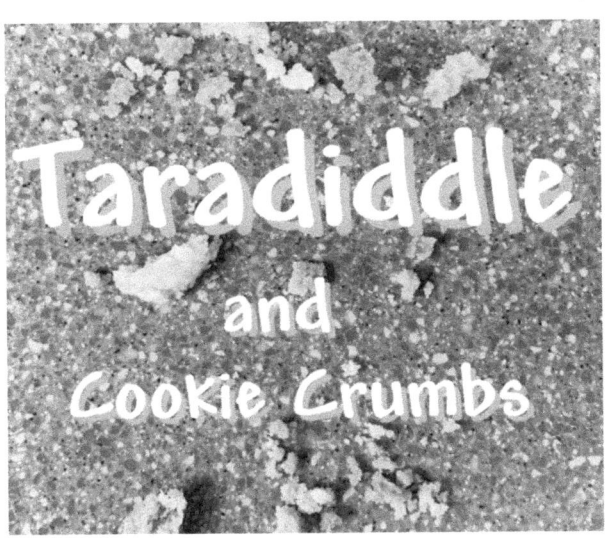

Other books by Richard Allen Anderson

Illustrated for Children:

The Adventures of Diggerydoo and Taller Too
Vabella Publishing, 2016

Poetry Collections:

Winter Weeds
Vabellla Publishing, 2019

Potholes in Memory Lane
Vabella Publishing, 2016

Another Season Spent
Vabella Publishing, 2013

Richard Allen Anderson

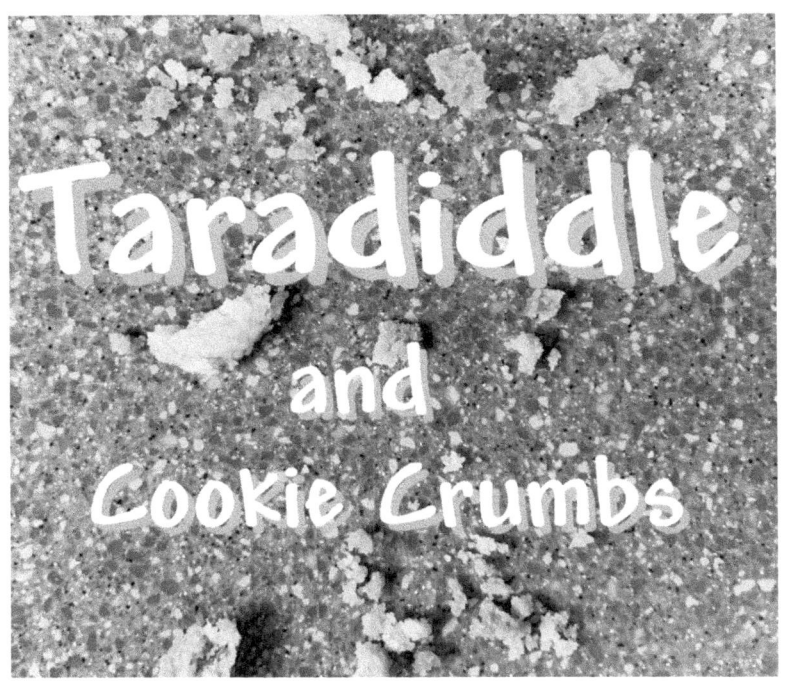

Vabella Publishing
P.O. Box 1052
Carrollton, Georgia 30112
www.vabella.com

Manufactured in the United States of America

13-digit ISBN 978-1-942766-63-6

Library of Congress Control Number 2019950959

10 9 8 7 6 5 4 3 2 1

This book is dedicated to all my fellow liars.

CONTENTS

Trinkett didn't sleep late. Her 327 citizens weren't that kind. Dawn till dark, mind your own business, "see y'all at church Sunday" folks are what they were—for the most part. They parked their aged-to-perfection Ford sedans and Chevy pickups in gravel drives under broad white oaks, tall cottonwoods or graceful willows next to the neat, covered porches of the white frame homes that lined the short lanes off Main Street.

Main Street cut Trinkett in half and fronted her few, small businesses. A 1944 John Deere stood on the flat roof of *Jake's Tool and Tractor Repair* across from *Maude's on Main*. *Big Wally's Cans and Coveralls* general store sported the only pane glass window front in town. The big windows reflected the hand-lettered *Bargain Antiques* sign propped against the open tables of Meg Williamson's perpetual flea market across the road, near the main intersection.

A few in town, like Maysie June Treadwell and her cousin Sissy McGovern, worked three days a week at the SmartMart, twenty miles west. Most all the town population got there too, at least once a month for their big shopping. SmartMart had everything anyone could ever need, except maybe a coffin.

Most were living out their retirement from farming or factory jobs in the drowsy town, quietly tending their gardens, phoning their adult children, checking their small savings accounts or taking advantage of the town's meager cultural opportunities.

The library upstairs from Maude's diner offered a large, if dated, collection of well-read, recycled paperbacks and magazines. No need for a librarian to manage the borrow-and-bring-back system, but old widow Shakelmeyer came in faithfully on Wednesdays to straighten up, even though, what with the stairs and all, she wasn't sure how much longer she could continue.

The quilting club membership was down to five of the town's women. They hadn't completed a quilt in two years, but that really wasn't the point, was it? Membership and attendance in the r.o.m.e.o. club (retired old men eating out) was variable, but the group occupied most of the tables at Maude's for mid-morning coffee, gossip and exchange of memories from better times.

Summer softball games in the mowed field behind the volunteer fire station turned out most of the town as did Sunday worship. Most everyone except Dr. Wright, the uppity retired professor who inherited Donald and Dearie's house a few years back, gathered to hear The Word followed by the latest news with coffee and doughnuts in Fellowship Hall after the service. Then home again by noon for an afternoon of television sports or raking leaves or such.

Though it lacked a charter, Trinkett was proud to have a mayor and two elected councilmen—honorary positions that served without pay and had few defined duties. It had law enforcement too, though, Lord knows, there had been no crime in town as long as anyone could remember.

~

On this day, most had already dropped seed for Speckle-Sweet corn, Harvest-Queen limas and Blue English Peas in their large, fenced gardens. The cautious would wait another week or two before planting the

Bumper-Boy tomatoes and Green or Golden-Wonder Peppers. Frost might still come to southern Illinois.

The faint streaks of dawn faded in the brightening morning sky. Ms. Markley Harrington of 13 Green Street, urged Hillie, her cosseted dachshund, to complete her early morning duty on the lawn of Maysie June Treadwell, 15 Green Street. Hillie jumped sideways and yapped shrilly at the forsythia bush near Treadwell's curb, too excited to squat and pee.

"Hush!" Ms. Harrington hissed and reached to pull the dog from under the fountain of yellow branches. She touched the cold dead face of her neighbor. She glimpsed the twisted mouth, frozen in a silent scream of shock and pain. "Maysie June," she shrieked. She recoiled from the dead hands reaching out in stiffened claws. She wet her pants and fled the grisly scene, dripping home to gasp her gory discovery to the 911 operator.

One block north, a Harvey Blake Transport truck rolled cautiously down Main, the only street in town with a street light. Truckers could save miles and minutes using the Trinkett shortcut, but they had learned long ago that Trinkett was a speed trap. Newcomers, before their enlightenment, paid for this knowledge with "fines" extracted from them by the local law, cash only, paid directly to one of the two town cops. Entering town via county highway Z, they geared their big rigs down to a crawl, carefully adhering to the posted 20 MPH limit. Loaded with corn for the ethanol still, merchandise for the SmartMart store, sugar-beets, soybeans or any manner of payload, the early morning traffic sent rumbles of jake-brakes, grinding of gears and clanging of cargos down each branching side street, alerting sleepy residents to a new day.

Harvey Blake ground the gears on his semi, a flatbed hauling long I-beams from the Illinois-Central Mill for a distant bridge project, and crept toward the stop at the edge of town where Main continued again as County Z. There he would carefully come to a complete stop before accelerating toward Interstate 64.

A lone figure stood in shadows, waiting at the final stop, glancing frequently back toward the quiet town. He wore faded denim jeans and huddled within an oversized wool coat, even though the spring morning carried a promise of summer. He dragged his left leg, shuffling in slow, tight circles, watching the sun ascending into the clear sky.

When he heard the groan and grind of changing gears of Blake's eighteen-wheeler, he limped forward to the roadside, cautious, thumb eagerly extended, waiting for the big rig to make its inevitable stop before escaping to the open road. He watched the truck shape grow and become distinct, until it finally wheezed and throbbed to a stop a few feet in front of him. When the driver waved an invitation to climb aboard, he struggled up the tractor's side and swung open the passenger door.

Harvey Blake recognized then that the small, frail figure was not a boy, as he had thought, but a man,—forty, maybe fifty. The man's head was lowered, his eyes shielded by the long bill of a weathered Cubs baseball cap.

Blake asked, "Where you heading?"

"North Caroline." The clenched lips scarcely moved in reply.

"Long way," the trucker offered, "I can get you most way there."

"What's your name?" he asked, hoping perhaps for diversion from the empty hours on the road ahead. He glanced toward his passenger but recoiled involuntarily from the sight of a raging, vacant eye socket that seemed to return his own quickly-diverted gaze more piercingly than any living eye could.

The hoarse whisper from his dark passenger was short and final, signaling the end of conversation. "Lazarus," the thin mouth in the grotesquely scarred face replied.

~

A pensive, Mona Lisa smile tugged gently at the corners of Mary MacNearny's lips as she hung Ben's uniform jacket in the closet. *I should pick up a storage bag for this. I bet Big Wally in Trinkett has one.* She pulled a light blue sport shirt from a hanger and laid it on the bed, still rumpled from their pre-dawn love making. She smoothed the open collar of the sport shirt. She had wanted and waited for this day for Ben and herself for so long. *Is our time really here at last?* This day would be the start their new life.

Mary MacNearny had not visited Trinkett more than a handful of times in her lifetime. Except for official police business, the same was true for Ben. Few of their kind did so without good reason to be there.

Neither Trinkett nor police business were in Ben's mind this morning as he showered. No need to hurry, he let the warm water play on his still-firm body, soothing away some of his perpetual aches. And, the Guardian was stocked, gassed up and ready for them to hit the open road, no definite destination in mind. He hoped Mary was as eager and happy as he was.

He heard the bedroom phone's muted ring and Mary hurrying to snatch it up before the third ring, to squelch any intrusion on their plans for the day. *Can't be Dispatch,* he thought, *they know my leave starts today. Be damned if we cancel it again!* But he rinsed quickly and stepped out of the stall onto the rag-rug shower mat.

Naked and dripping, he took the cordless that his wife held out without comment but with that look that meant Trouble with a capital T. "Deputy Sheriff MacNearny," he rasped, forcing his mind into focus for the call.

"Wake up Mac! This is Peggy at Dispatch."

"I'm awake. You know I'm on leave, Peg. This better be good news about my retirement."

"They need you in Trinkett, Mac. Now. There's been a murder."

"Murder in Trinkett?" He watched Mary raise her hand and shake her head, mouthing the words "No. No."

"Damn, Peg, we're leaving in the motor home right after breakfast. Call the Trinkett PD—whasisname—Crutch—or, uh, Tank? Let 'em do something for their pay, for once."

"Seems they can't find neither one; probably off fishing. Tank's supposed to be on duty, but he ain't around nowhere. Crutch neither. Sheriff's gone to Kankakee for some big meeting—so move your old black ass, darling, 'cause the good citizens of Trinkett need help, and you're it."

MacNearny cursed, wanting to hurl the phone at the wall, then said "I'll get there soon's I can." He turned to face his wife, standing arms akimbo at his side. She took the phone from his hands silently with a glare that stopped any words of explanation before they left his mouth. He turned away and grabbed a towel from the bathroom, though his dark skin was nearly dry now. He scrubbed the towel over the nap of his short-cropped, graying hair and watched Mary turn her back and stalk away.

Ben retrieved his gray county sheriff's uniform and dressed quickly, trying to ignore the sport shirt Mary had put out for him on the bed. He decided to travel light and strapped on the service belt that held only his old S&W police-special revolver and one cuff holder. He stuck a slim, eight-inch, leaded leather slapper in his rear pants pocket and a small notepad and pencil in the shirt pocket behind his badge. Finally, he placed the cap squarely on his head, the insignia facing exactly front and center, checked himself in the full-length mirror and strode, ready and erect, to the back door.

Mary sat at the kitchen table. She did not bother to ask if he wanted coffee before he left, or even to look in his direction. He spoke to her back. "I'm sorry, babe. I have to go. There's no one else."

No answer. "Godamn, Mary, it's a killing. We can still leave later when I get this taken care of . . . but . . . I have to go!"

Mary, who always understood, always gave her blessings for his safety, never allowed him to leave without a buzz on his cheek or a pat on his ass, remained distracted by the wrens building a nest outside the bay window, just under the eave.

Ben stepped out and quietly pulled the door shut behind him. He walked past the Guardian motorhome, loaded and ready in the driveway to start their month of freedom and exploration. He slid into the dark brown police cruiser and jammed the key at the ignition. He was not a happy camper.

From his home near Olney, the county seat, Trinkett was a short thirty-minute drive on quiet, country roads. MacNearny usually enjoyed the leisurely drive on those rare occasions when he went there, but this time he pushed the gas pedal hard as he guided the heavy vehicle past fields of emerging crops and greening pastures. And he thought of the last time he'd made the trip—last fall when the fields were brown and the Indian almost died.

~

The Indian was a "breed" from eastern Oklahoma, though even his blood brothers took him for full-blooded Cherokee. His skin had the color of cured tobacco. His flowing hair was black as ravens' wings. It hung untamed to his shoulders or pulled back in a tail in hot weather. His fierce eyes, set wide in his hawkish face over prominent cheekbones, belied a gentle nature. In profile his angular nose and rock jaw were classic Indian. His dress in all seasons was dungarees and a plaid wool shirt— conventional country except for the red turban he wore from time to time in place of a more typical baseball cap or Stetson.

He arrived at Trinkett in mid-summer, hungry and on foot, a hitchhiker of freight trains, highway diesels, and the backs of pickup trucks. He had no cash, no credit, no acquaintance. The clothes he'd stolen after breaking out of jail hung too large on him, hiding his lean, tightly muscled frame.

He sat below the *Help Wanted* sign that hung on the high chain-link fence at Jackson's Junk Yard. The heavy, early morning air forecast a steamy afternoon. When Jackson arrived and unchained the gate, the Indian applied informally: "Name's Charley. I want the job. I can do 'most anything."

He accepted the wage of a dollar less than minimum as gratefully as the morning coffee Junk Jackson offered after they had sized each other up in the shack Junk called his office. Junk was happy to have some cheap labor for the harder work. Charley determined that he could take whatever Junk could dish out.

But by late afternoon, Charley felt weak and sick with hunger after twelve hours stripping car wrecks and learning to operate the massive hydraulic machine that compressed them to dense blocks of scrap metal. Jackson suggested, "Best hustle on down to see Maude before she closes."

Maude's Place on Main Street served Fairly Fast Food, as the sign painted on the front window proclaimed, from 7 AM until 7 PM every day but Sunday. Maude Kraft was just reaching to turn the window card from "Come On In" to "Sorry, We're Closed" when Charley walked in.

Reading from the chalkboard menu that listed but one choice, Charley ordered Number One: Meatloaf. Maude smiled and wondered, *What's a coyote like you doing in Trinkett?*

She said, "Okay, Stranger. You staying in town?" She looked past his worried smile, saw his hunger and loaded his plate with double meat, mashed potatoes, and veggie-combo, happy to find a home for the last of her offerings of the day.

"Workin' at Jackson's for a while. Gonna live in his old bus," Charley said. He wiped gravy from the corner of his mouth with the back of his hand and wondered if he should trust her. He waited until his plate was empty before he confessed, "Can't pay till Friday, ma'am."

"Call me Maude, and who might you be?" she said and slid a plate of strawberry pie in front of him.

~

To white acquaintances, his name was Charley Crow. His Native American tribesmen called him Tsali. To the patrons of Bailey's Bar he became Turban Charley, or just Turban. *Better than "Chief"*, he thought. The nickname was an honor unwittingly conferred by an instant bar-buddy. The red turban he sometimes wore was Charley's silent assertion of Cherokee pride.

Charley never drank more than one Coors Light draft, nursing it for an hour like a large, liquid hourglass that would signal his departure when he drained the last flat, warm drops. Bailey never minded. Charley was a welcome diversion for Bailey's patrons, entertaining them with jokes and legends and wonderful lies.

One late-September night, Charley dropped four quarters on the bar and told Bailey, "See you tomorrow." It was cool in the street. Dead leaves rustled and crunched underfoot—musty harbingers of winter. Charley turned up Green Street to return to Jackson's and bed down in the gutted bus that had been his home for the past two months. He stopped and jerked his forearm over his eyes when the spot light caught him in its blinding glare.

The light held him like an unwilling actor on stage, then suddenly it went out. A voice in the dark said, "Hold it right there, Injun Boy." It was a voice he had heard before, at the yard. It was Tank Jackson, Junk's younger brother.

Tank was dumb as a knob, obese as a brood sow and the day-shift half of the Trinkett PD. His nickname was a leftover from high school football days when, as offensive guard, he rolled over opposing linesmen like an M1A1 battle tank. He had savored the bruising contact, rejoiced in the occasional audible snapping of bones. Opponents eventually took a dive, rolled over, or stepped aside to avoid his attack. None challenged him and successfully avoided pain or injury. Tonight he rode with Sergeant Tom Crutch on night patrol, looking for a little amusement.

The prowl car doors opened. Tank squeezed out and lumbered toward Charley. Tom Crutch slid his six-foot-seven frame from behind the wheel, slow and lazy. His voice was a low, musical bass. "What you up to, Injun?" he said quietly.

Shit! Charley swore to himself before he answered carefully, "Heading home for the night, Sergeant, that's all . . . Sir." In the dim light he saw the long barrel of the shotgun sidearm Crutch always carried.

"You trying to be a smart ass?" Crutch said. The low voice now was flat and menacing.

Charley resisted running, fearing the shotgun. He stood still in the dark, eyes searching, squinting to focus on shadows. No one was on the street. Then he saw the woman on the porch stand up and move from the rocker to the porch railing. Something glinted in her hands, flashing, clicking. She was knitting—silently watching and listening—and knitting.

The double barrels of Crutch's weapon jabbed deep into Charley's gut, bent him over from the waist, and Charley lost the beer. "You botherin' Miz Treadwell?" Crutch demanded. "This Injun botherin' you, Maysie June?"

Silence from the porch except for the muted click, click, click and what might have been an excited squeal.

Charley took one step forward. The blue steel gun barrel flashed down, crushing his shoulder bone. "He's trying to run, Tank. Stomp him."

The beating did not take long. Although he remained conscious through all of it, Charley did not scream or call out for help. Had he stayed down, remained inert, he might have escaped with lesser injury. Each futile struggle to his feet or knees stimulated a fresh assault. In the end both his fibulas were cracked, yielding to a slashing nightstick or a well-placed kick. One kneecap was dislodged and his spleen was split, seeping blood and fluid inside his bruised belly.

Tank proudly stood aside for Crutch. Charley was defenseless on his knees and in shock. Crutch's blows cracked his skull, hammered his face, broke his cheekbone, nose and jaw. The final blow popped his left eye from its socket. It dangled loose on his battered face. He pitched forward, finally unconscious.

~

The next morning, Ben MacNearny had stopped at Olney County Hospital and Morgue to collect the Sheriff's Daily Summary Report. "Maybe you should wait until the boys get back from Trinkett," the hospital clerk suggested, "they're picking up a body. Sounds messy."

"Anyone I know?" the deputy asked, although he thought that unlikely. He had met Trinkett's boys in blue, Crutch and Jackson, at a law enforcement conference once, but none of his kith or kin had ever lived in their old, tight community.

"What I hear, they don't know who it is. No ID on the body, but had $300 cash still in his pocket. Some woman called it in real early—wouldn't give her name or anything. They should be back here soon. Pull up a chair."

MacNearny checked his Timex and moved toward the exit. "I'd best get to work." He had parked the cruiser near the emergency door. He found the ambulance idling there, blocking his exit. The EMTs rushed past him, pushing the Gurney toward the ER. One of them glanced up, wide-eyed with amazement, and said, "He's not dead, but he ought to be."

The deputy was surprised to learn a week later that the unidentified victim still lived, but no police action had been taken. That's when his instincts directed him to take an unofficial interest, and he started checking at the hospital occasionally, then regularly. Day after day, the victim's chart didn't change as he hung on to life by a tenuous but tenacious thread.

Weeks crawled by before the victim would yield a set of fingerprints. He lay in a coma while surgeons discussed if and how to repair his broken body. They drained his blood-soaked gut and removed the ruptured spleen. His eye could not be saved or re-inserted. Not expecting the victim to survive, they allowed the empty socket to close and heal over, leaving a vicious, flaming scar. They set the major bone fractures but postponed the delicate face surgery, pending a return to consciousness, while they wagered on his chance of survival.

Meanwhile, MacNearny brought Polaroid snapshots of the victim to Trinkett. Maude Kraft looked long and hard at the bandaged head before she said, "That's Charley. I'm sure—yes it's him. We thought he'd just drifted on again. My God, what happened to his face?"

Others, at Bailey's, verified her identification, "Yeah, sure . . . that's Turban—Turban Charley." Sergeant Crutch offered that the bus where Charley had lived yielded nothing to reveal Charley's home or background. "We don't know where the greasy little prick was from," he said, "no big loss."

Ms. Treadwell had flushed with excitement when Ben questioned her. Her knitting needles clicked erratically, stopped, labored on. She said, "I retired early that night, Sheriff. Slept like a babe. Didn't hear nothing, didn't see nothing, don't know nothing." She licked a drop of nervous sweat from a plump lip and asked in a low whisper, "He ain't going to live, is he?"

The FBI office in Chicago mailed their make on Turban Charley's fingerprints to Deputy MacNearny. *Charles Woodrow Crow . . . Felony rape . . . convicted in Oklahoma . . . imprisoned two years ago . . . escaped this July.*

Ben folded the report into his uniform pocket and called County Hospital. "Guess what," the ward nurse said, "his good eye is open. Don't know if he sees anything, and he's sure not talking. Still sleeps a lot. No sign that he's aware where he is or that he just spent three months unconscious."

When Ben MacNearny spent New Year's Day at Charley's bedside, Mary remarked, only half joking, "I don't know who you love more, me or that Indian." Ben sat with feet up, head back, alternately napping and reviewing the past weeks in his mind. He had by now spent many hours of many days at Charley's side waiting to learn if a mind still functioned in the broken skull. He needed to know who had done this, who had punished and broken this man.

Is this retribution for your crimes, Charley Crow? Who else could have hated you enough to do this? Or maybe you just ain't the right color. I know you're not much to be proud of Mr. Crow, but I don't figure you deserved this. No way!

Charley's eye was closed. His breathing was so shallow that Ben bent toward the bed to listen carefully for breathing. Then he spoke softly, as if disclosing a secret to the sleeping man, "Six months, Charley, six months more and my retirement is vested. Mary and me, we're taking a trip this spring to look for our retirement home. Hope to hell you die or come awake soon, 'cause I'm gone then, and nobody's gonna give a damn who done this to you."

Ben saw Charley's eye open and finally focus on his uniform. He watched the pillowed head twist and recoil in terror. The broken jaws struggled to open, to scream a protest or perhaps a curse, but only a pained, protracted groan escaped. He waited quietly while the victim's eye furtively closed and reopened, searching the sterile room—fearful, questioning.

He whispered into Charley's ear. "Tell me who did this." It was a demand he would utter many times in the following days, always with the same response—the slow, negative twist of Charley's head from side to side.

When Charley was able to sit up in bed, Ben confronted him with the FBI report. Again the slow headshake of denial. He held Charley's tortured face in his big hand to prevent him from turning away and growled, "Damn it man, how can I help you if you won't talk?" To himself he wondered how long Charley would survive, if he could heal enough to go back into prison.

~

Now as he approached Trinkett, MacNearney decided against using the car's siren or the carnival lights—no need to get the whole town in an uproar. He knew though that before tomorrow all 327—or maybe now it was down to 326—residents of the close-knit town would know as much or more than he did. Every mouth would speak the news; every ear would hear it.

He channeled his thoughts to the trip he and Mary were supposed to be starting today. Mary had planned it for a year, ever since the possibility of his retirement seemed real: a month-long trip to visit new places far from Olney and the Sheriff's office, a month to look over communities for their retirement days together. Pleasant thoughts and plans that he, too, eagerly anticipated, yet he flushed with guilt when he recognized that Charley Crow would be abandoned to his uncertain fate with the Indian's tormentors left undetected and unpunished.

He recalled when Charley had finally spoken to him. In painful words, slow and determined, he had spoken first of the land of his ancestors, the mountains and streams of the Great Smokey Mountains where good spirits fly on eagles' wings. He had clutched Mac's hand, grasping for his attention and compelling their eyes to meet.

He spoke his denial once only, "The rape was another man's crime, not mine."

Outside the winter wind sifted light snow past the hospital room's small window. Charley lifted a hand to his broken face and said, "For this, justice will be done." It was not a plea, not a question. It was a statement, an assurance to the man at his side, the man he had learned to trust with the turning of the seasons, the gentle man with a heart as fierce as his own.

MacNearny turned the cruiser onto Main Street and parked at City Hall. He needed to find Tom Crutch or Tank Jackson for more information on the reported homicide. He had listened to the hysterical, recorded 911 call, and Peggy had read him the coroner's initial report on last night's victim. It was the Treadwell woman, the one he'd questioned months ago about Charley's assault and battery. She had died during the dark, transitional minutes near midnight. She died with a giant knitting needle piercing the muscles of her heart, skewered through from chest to back like a plump kabob.

Ben forced himself out of the car. It was one of those days when every accumulated ache of sixty years came to haunt him. He was tired—weary of crime and criminals, weary of high-speed chases, weary of confronting danger from punks and perps, weary of attempting to correct life's injustices, weary of imperfect systems and of evil people.

He trudged into City Hall and found the mayor's office. Junk Jackson was inside, shouting at the mayor, wild-eyed, a blubbering hulk, "Jesus, Jesus, oh, holy fucking Jesus!" Ben straightened up and paused at the office door.

The mayor asked, "You *sure* it's Tank?"

Junk looked pale. "Christ, it's him! Couldn't tell except for the hand hanging by a sliver from the window. He's mashed. All guts and broken bones and bloody flesh inside his car. Run through the crusher." He retched and puked his morning meal over the waxed hardwood floor.

MacNearny didn't wait for more. He jerked around and jogged down the hall, out of the building and across the still-dormant lawn. He was wheezing and sweating in the warm spring air when he reached for the cruiser's radiophone. Half of the local law enforcement had just shown up dead! He needed County backup quickly. He called the Sheriff's hot line first and got no answer. He called County Hospital. "No, the Sheriff isn't here. Think he had business in Kankakee, didn't he?"

Shit, that's right, Peggy told me that. He almost missed the voice on the radiophone continuing, "By the way, your friend, Charley Crow, is missing; we think he left last night sometime . . . somehow."

Damn! Anything else? I don't need any of this before I retire. I don't need it any damned time! Why the hell didn't the Sheriff handle this, and where the hell is Crutch, damn him? He slammed the car into drive, ran a U-turn over both curbs and headed for the Trinkett police garage.

He jerked to a stop outside the closed overhead door and quickly walked to the side entrance. That's odd, the patrol car is here. The trunk of the car stood ajar just enough he knew it wasn't shut. Mac's hand shook. From the instinct bred of thirty years of police work, he sensed trouble. His temples pounded as he reached to open the unlocked trunk.

Crutch's long frame was twisted and crumpled inside. The left side of his face had been blown away by a shotgun blast at short range. A single fly buzzed and landed to explore the savage wound. Crutch's prized sidearm, the double-barreled ten-gauge, lay at his side carefully wrapped in a red turban.

He whispered through his clenched teeth. "Jesus, Charley why didn't you just carve your initials in his forehead?" He wiped down the long gun barrel, stock and trigger with the turban. *So these are the bastards that crippled you. And this is your Cherokee justice. But why* the Treadwell woman? His thoughts raced. *She watched it all didn't she! I knew she wasn't clean.*

He unconsciously folded the turban and stuffed it into the pocket of his uniform jacket. *How did you manage it, Charley, you could hardly walk? You won't last a week outside the hospital.*

Driving home, he wondered how he was going to tell Mary. *What can I say to her? How can I explain what this means to me, to us?* He didn't know with certainty what was coming next himself, but he knew he couldn't leave now until this matter was laid to rest, maybe not for a month, maybe not for a year.

He jammed his hand inside his jacket pocket and found the red turban. *Way to go Ben, you dumb fuck, way to go. Now you're removing evidence from a capital crime scene.* But he knew he wouldn't turn the turban in. He knew he would destroy it. He knew he would oversee the continued investigation in Trinkett. He had already discredited a report to the mayor that someone resembling Turban Charley had been seen boarding a Blake Transit truck that morning at the edge of town, heading east.

Ben knew that only he knew what Charley had done. No one else would believe it possible. But Deputy Benjamin MacNearny knew, and he would have to stick around to make sure that the case eventually went into the *Unsolved* file.

Long shadows of the row of young, slender maples crossed the road like giant prison bars when he finally wheeled the cruiser into his driveway. Ben knew then that he would not have to worry what to say to Mary now.

The Guardian was gone.

~

Cold gripped the summit of Chiltoes Mountain at 5000 feet. Charley Crow sat looking out at the mist of morning vapors that gave the Great Smokys their name. The sun climbed out of the valley and lighted his face. His vision faded as he fought to focus on nearby blossoms of rhododendron and mountain laurel. His eye strained to watch an eagle float on giant wings and come to roost on a broken branch atop the skeleton of a tall, dead fir tree.

Charley was drained, every reserve of energy spent on his mission of justice, his flight cross-country and his long climb to face the sun—and die. A feeble smile lighted his somber face, and he spoke to the eagle, "Greetings my free, feathered brother."

The eagle turned his head and called, "Tsali, Tsali, Tsali."

Strudeloo

I love strudel. It is one of humankind's finest achievements. But then, I am partial to apples, one of my own better works. We go way back together, back to that prehistoric garden with its primitive flora and fauna, the ancestral humans, the apple and me.

I mentioned this to old Jake not long ago. We had quite a little discussion. The last day he came into my shop. Just before he died.

I do not talk with many without my earthly guise, and then, only just before they die. They really cannot tell me anything I do not know, of course, but I like sometimes to hear their own words, their deepest thoughts expressed. I credit their development of a human language right up there with strudel. What do they think of me? And of all the rest? From their own minds. From their own lips.

Often they are skeptical or confused by their fright, once they have an inkling of who I am. I try to break it to them slowly. When they overcome that, or accept that, it pleases them greatly to speak with me. They feel singled out and special, no longer threatened. Honored, often. Humans are funny that way—egos demeaned or enhanced by association. I usually know what to expect. Not always.

Not with Jake. Jake got pissed. Really pissed. That's what killed him, with his fragile heart. I knew it would.

~

"Guten Morgen Herr Gottlieb. Are you so busy now?"

"Not at all, Jake. I have all the time in the world . . . especially when you come with strudel! Sit. I will brew some fresh coffee for us."

"Coffee will be good. I cannot warm up today."

21

He hobbled slowly into the alcove where I displayed the best examples of my carvings in the shop window. He carried a brown bag to the small corner table and sat in one of the wooden chairs, looking out to the deserted street. His frail body was almost lost within the heavy folds of his woolen overcoat. The morning sun flooded the alcove, illuminating him like a stage light. It seemed to warm him a little. His watery eyes, framed by the visor of his dark wool cap and the gray stubble on his chin, peered out without expression.

"Warm yourself in the sun, Jake. It is such a beautiful day. I will bring cups and plates. Did you see the daffodils in front of the playhouse? Aren't they a welcome sight?"

I brought two dishes to the table. I removed the strudels from the bag and placed one on each plate. They were still warm and smelled heavenly.

"The snow is almost gone," Jake said. "Dress rehearsals for the play are starting already." He dabbed at his eyes with the worn sleeve of his coat. "I don't think . . . I will see the play this year." He spoke haltingly, as if unwilling or fearful to speak the words.

Jake was right. He would not see the Passion Play. He would not see tomorrow. Still, I humored him, tried to divert his thoughts. "You have been in every performance for the past eighty years, Jake. You were just a child in 1930, your first play. No play in 1940. The war was raging. But since then, how many more? Seven more, right? You should be proud."

"Half of the village will be in the play. More than 2000. I'm nothing special"

"But, you could play any role, Jake. Did you ever play Jesus?"

"God, no. Too hard! Too much work. Too much emotion. Judas maybe would be better. Most often I am just one of the crowd . . . calling for crucifixion."

Jake is wrong, I thought. It is easier to be a deity than to be human.

I said, "A few visitors have already arrived. Soon they will fill the inns. Before fall, hundreds of thousands from all over the globe will overrun our small village. You will not be able to walk in the streets. The merchants will be rich again for a few months."

"And you will sell many wood carvings to the pilgrims—the tourists." He winked and smiled wryly. "All this hubbub because the people are so moved by this old myth. Not long now, it will be 400 years since the first play . . . 400 years, but too late for me to enjoy the celebrations, I'm afraid."

The espresso machine hissed like an angry viper, and I left Jake to his thoughts. I added cream and hot water to the thick, dark brew and brought two forks with the two steaming cups to the table. Jake warmed his bony hands on the hot china, held it to his face and breathed in the rich aroma.

"I would like sugar today," he said. "What do you think of the myth, Gottlieb?"

"Well, it is a beautiful story, isn't it? And more enduring than most myths. A wonderful conception. The son of a god who sacrifices himself to give humanity everlasting life."

Old Jake stirred another spoonful of sugar into his coffee. "The people living here are dedicated to the play. It brings much money to our small village. We would be unknown without it. You have lived here even longer than I, Herr Gottlieb. But you have said that you were not born here. Why did you settle here in Oberammergau? Was it the play?"

"Yes, Jake. But that's not the complete answer. I live here because this is one of the most beautiful places on this planet. In the universe, really. I like it here. The mountains inspire me, the winter snows, the icy rushing waters in the spring. Even the sudden storms with lightning flashes and thunder shaking the ground—all of nature's wonders.

"But most of all, I am here because of the people. The play interests me, but more than that, it brings men and women and children of many countries to my door."

Jake's tremulous hands brought the cup to his lips, and he sipped the hot liquid carefully. "Where else have you lived?" he asked. "It seems you have been here always."

"I have been here always, but I have lived everywhere. I am the creator. I am omnipresent and omniscient." I answered Jake's questions with direct truths, though I knew he was not yet prepared to understand. His troubled eyes blinked with confusion.

"Here, let me help you cut your strudel," I said, and divided his last treat into small pieces. "Best to take this a small bit at a time."

Jake ate, and said, "I know you are a creator, Gottlieb. You have an unearthly talent to create beautiful, magical carvings. Wondrous carvings. All the plants and animals. All the beauty of nature. Everyone says they have never seen anything like your work, ever. Men, women, children—you render them beautifully. But always with a tiny, unobtrusive yet observable flaw. It's like your trademark. Why, Gottlieb?"

"Not all of my creations have been so marvelous as my carvings, Jake. I never seem to get it right the first time. Not to worry, though. There is plenty of time for more experiments. Plenty of time to seek perfection, if such a thing can be achieved . . . or even defined. How will we know it then?"

Jake stopped chewing, puzzled. He drained his coffee, and sat silent for a moment. At last he asked, "Are you talking about creation . . . or evolution?"

"Well, both. It is all one process, really. Your scientists and historians have discovered how your own species and many others have changed even as far back as millions of years. And you are beginning to understand the mysteries of the infinite universe. Very commendable"

"You agree with Darwin?" Jake asked, "the survival of the fittest?"

"Not entirely. It does explain the natural adaptations that occur without my intervention. Not all of my imposed changes have been improvements. I have made some colossal mistakes, Jake. I suppose I should apologize to someone. But to whom?"

I had to laugh at my own small joke before I chose to reveal myself fully to Jake's mind. He understood immediately, without intimidation or fear. He said, "Mistakes? God does not make mistakes!"

"Oh, my dear old fellow, you are so wrong. To err is human, true enough. It is the path of progress. But I too have made grievous errors. Take the dinosaurs, for example. I thought they were magnificent when I started out with them. I created one model after the other— hundreds of them. But, there were many design flaws that showed up in far future generations. Meanwhile, the planet itself changed, eon upon eon. Finally, I realized even the basic concept did not make sense anymore."

I paused to sip my coffee, observing Jake through the rim of the cup.

"The planet itself was evolving. This tiny fragment in an evolving universe undergoing colossal change. Nature alone would never be able to adapt the magnificent monsters or eliminate new species that had begun to compete with them. I had to interfere. So I destroyed them. Killed the whole experiment and annihilated every single one. It was fast and merciful . . . as much as possible."

Jake stretched a bony finger in my direction. "You can't be God! Show me a sign. Prove yourself," he shouted, wanting to be convinced of the truth he already knew.

"Oh, Jake, please be calm. You do not need some magical legerdemain to know me. There have been many errors. I do the best job I can, but I am not infallible, as some of you think. Evolution is my ace in the hole. I do not like to interfere with its gradual progress. Still, there were times I had to obliterate entire eons of development. Had to erase and step backward. Take my ice ages. My glaciers succeeded in wiping out many unsatisfactory species . . . some experimental forms that I since abandoned."

Jake's troubled eyes stared at me in wonder. I continued.

"Humans survived though . . . an early primitive model, to be sure. I could not speak with them as I am with you. Their thoughts were primordial, without words to express them, and I terrified them to death. Eventually, they invented their own gods to help explain the unexplainable. I didn't mind."

Curiosity had subdued Jake's anger and fear. "Why are you telling me this?" he demanded.

"You are the wisest man I know, Jake. You are educated and know the things of which I speak. And you are dying, you know that too. You are not the only one. Next week I will ask young Mrs. Schmidler to talk with me, just before her time comes. She has a good mind and is more thoughtful than most. And she is a mother."

Jake looked at me skeptically, but said nothing. Maybe this was too much for him after all, too much mental and emotional challenge for his aged mind and heart.

Still, I pressed on. "To tell the truth, I have been thinking of redirecting the next stage of human evolution— or maybe even starting over, going back to square one. Human development proceeded quite nicely until recently, I think. Not long after the early humans came down out of the trees, their bodies began to change. Their minds developed too. They discovered how cooperative efforts could benefit them. They gathered into tribes—extended families. But they learned to make war too, killing those they saw as different, killing to protect their own kind. I did not step in."

Jake said abruptly, "So, what is your point? They were more animal than human. All animals protect their own."

"Soon they went beyond animal behavior. They created primitive religions and many gods, adaptations of their own image. They sacrificed humanity in the name of religious beliefs and transgressed against fellow humans for the sake of their imagined gods."

"Yes, we appealed to something outside ourselves, bigger than ourselves, for defense from nature's fearsome forces. . . call them gods if you like."

Jake took the offensive. "We continued to learn. Those primeval minds developed. Intellect dominated physical superiority. We built shelters, then cities . . . universities . . . libraries of accumulated knowledge—astonishing accomplishments, you must agree. Knowledge became our unending goal and our new salvation. 'Ignorance is the curse of God, knowledge the wing wherewith we fly to heaven.' The bard said that. You must agree?"

"Yes, Jake. You began learning the secrets of the earth and of the universe—my secrets. You went beyond learning. You created from your knowledge, like me, the only animal species able to do so. But often you have used your knowledge to self-destruct. You have turned against your own species—killing, destroying those cities that hundreds of generations built. You have destroyed whole populations, the only animal species to do so."

Jake remained silent but intensely alert. I pressed on. "You have used your hard-won knowledge to bring benefits that I had hardly imagined to this small world, but in your greed for riches and power you have also endangered all the species that inhabit it. You have carelessly usurped the riches of the earth and ignored the onset of catastrophic environmental changes resulting from your human activities. You have built more and more powerful weapons of war. You do not require my help now to annihilate your entire species and many others that innocently share this planet with you."

Jake brought up a thin, veined hand in silent protest. I made a final point. "Maybe the experiment to allow you to populate and evolve freely has gone too far." Jake's hand dropped to the table. His head hung forward. I could not see his face. "Perhaps there is some genetic flaw. . . I do not know what to do."

Jake raised his head. Color had come into his wan and wizened face. Fire lighted his weary eyes. "But Gott im himmel!" he squealed, "What of the good? You gave us disease and disability. Were these some of your damned mistakes? We have conquered many of these. Eventually all of them will fall. Did you help us then? You allow the good to die young and the evil to persist amongst us. So we try to help ourselves, seeking new knowledge for understanding and control. We call it science. Others pray, believing you have an interest in their welfare. Still others devise laws that seek justice. And at times we must go to war against the evil some have allowed to flourish."

He sank back with a sigh and continued calmly now. "Do you think we are just an experiment that you can tamper with if it does not please you . . . when you think you have made a mistake? How can you condemn our mistakes then? How can you expect more from us?"

He struggled on, his voice faded to a hoarse whisper. "Men and women have given up their lives reaching out for new knowledge, but you do not permit us to understand our very existence. If you do not know our purpose and our end, how can we? Damn your experiments! What kind of fiend are you? "

Jake slumped forward, knocking his empty cup to the floor. His head fell between his two arms spread upon the tabletop, reaching in my direction. Reaching out for me.

I picked the espresso cup and some strudel crumbs off the floor and cleaned the table. I moved to the shop door and opened it. The air was fresh with the smell of spring rain moving down from the mountains. A young family crossed the street. The man was tall, with sturdy legs and a strong chest. He was dressed in the costume of an ancient Roman soldier. His frau and two young kinder were costumed also, wearing plain, flowing robes of biblical times. They walked quickly, intent on appearing on time for the first dress rehearsal of the play.

"Please come," I called out. "Please help. My friend has died."

The children looked up at their parents. The man paused for a moment to look at me. The woman grasped the children's hands. The busy family hurried away as rain began to fall. Suddenly, the wind increased, howling and swirling wildly down the narrow street. I watched as lightning struck the breastplate of the ersatz Roman soldier, killing him in an agonizing flash.

~

Note: The Oberammergau Passion Play was first performed in 1634 as an appeasement and appeal to God to spare the village from the plague that was killing thousands across Europe. The village was spared, and the play, a five hour enactment of the life and death of Christ, continues to be performed to this day, now on even decades. Most of the town residents are involved in the extravagant productions. Hundreds of thousands of visitors crowd the tiny Bavarian village during the year the play is performed. Many leave with one of the wood carvings for which the town is also noted.

Passage

The man was tall and thin, and his steps were slow. He did not recognize this dark valley or the path he walked upon. His mind was calm and clear, but oddly vacant. Few thoughts disturbed his peaceful mood; no images played before his mind's eye.

He had come onto the path in the midst of dense fog, uncertain how he had come here, uncertain how to proceed. He started to walk, hesitating, eyes fixed a few feet ahead on the path, his legs weak, his step unsteady.

Vague thoughts surfaced slowly as he walked— pleasant recollections of a recent farewell, of warm hands and voices, of surrendering to some strange new force that had brought him here to this dark, fog-shrouded pathway.

~

The little dog waited patiently through dimensionless waves of time. She was small with flowing black hair and big, floppy ears. No playmates occupied her attention or eased her lonely vigil, and yet, she was content. Her long, bushy tail wagged expectantly from time to time, confident that her faithful watch would somehow be fulfilled.

At times, her sharp hearing detected distant voices, happy voices. She stood and faced the sound, prancing around in happy circles until the voices faded again. No man, woman or child passed along the path that crossed the bottom of the hillock where she lay.

Now, she lay still, docile and patient, watching with sleepy eyes but alert for any new sound or scent.

~

Continuing his slow pace up the gradual slope, the man's vision improved, or was it only that the fog was thinning? He lifted his gaze to look farther ahead. Was there sunlight in the distance, an end to the fog? A slight breeze ruffled wisps of his sparse gray hair and brought hints of fragrance to his nostrils. Feeling stronger, he increased his pace. His weakened legs did not resist but responded with renewed vigor.

Bits of scenery appeared around him now, shrubs and flowers in banks along the quiet pathway, reminders of someplace he had known before. He recognized some as familiar favorites—bright crocus, tulips and iris in varying shades and hues. They seemed to shine with an unearthly beauty.

Cheered, but still unaware of his destination, unease and uncertainty slowly abated. He began to feel welcome and secure in this strangely quiet and unfamiliar place. His spirits rose. Fragments of memory from another time, another place, gently entered his mind.

~

The small dog's ears perked and she jumped to her paws, sniffing the still air and watching. There in the distance, walking steadily toward her on the path, a man approached. She knew this man. She took one leap forward, then stopped and cocked her head, one ear up, the other hanging loose. She watched cautiously and sniffed again. Now she was certain. A short white beard camouflaged the familiar face, but she knew the man. She ran toward him, tail and tongue wagging happily.

~

The man walked erect now as the sun warmed his face. Random visions played in his mind. He saw a dog running toward him as in a dream. But the dog was real. He knew this dog.

"Beanie!" he said, though he knew not how the name came to him. He dropped to one knee. The dog pranced up and licked his face and yapped with joy. "Oh, Beanie," he said, and lifted her in his arms.

The man and dog walked on together. Neither felt hunger or fatigue, though the winding, hilly path appeared endless. Now and then the man stopped to gaze upon some new scene that opened around a curve in the path, scenes with a strange familiarity—a stand of tall pine trees, a peaceful blue lake, a quiet green meadow, a deep blue sky with rolling heaps of bright white clouds.

He stopped to sit on a large, flat rock next to a pool of cool, clear water. The dog drank, then jumped onto his lap. He scratched behind her ears as she lay quietly, joyfully fulfilled at last. Sitting there, other scenes took shape before him—shimmering mirages on the path, not fully distinct but still recognizable and welcome.

A white-haired woman stood alone, gazing from the window of a house onto a wide vista of green grass and trees. Unshed tears glistened in her eyes. That scene faded, replaced by another. The woman appeared younger now and busy with housewifely projects or tending some need of two young children who demanded her attention.

The man reached out to them as the vision faded and disappeared. He smiled and rose to continue on the path, the little dog ready to follow at his heels.

Man and dog walked on. His arms now swung briskly at his sides. His strides were strong. The dog ran off the path, investigating some intriguing diversion, then back again to her master's side. The path straightened.

Ahead, on the horizon, the man saw what appeared to be the tall, wide gates of a country manor. The gateway stood open, inviting them into a bright courtyard.

The man looked back at the trail he had walked. How long had it been—an hour, a day, a week? Time did not seem to matter. He turned again to face the gateway just ahead. What was this shining place? Was this his destination? Voices reached his ears. Were more reunions in store for them beyond these gates?

"Come, Beanie," he called, and they continued the passage.

Peach Trees and Priscilla's Porridge

"I can't believe the low price on this house. Four bedrooms. Five acres. A peach orchard."

Even while we dreamed of what our future together might be, we had longed for a little place in the county, a place to call our own, but over the years the dream had become dimmer and dimmer.

"Five acres at that price? Must be a misprint."

"Well, let's call. Let's take a look. For fun, at least. Oh, I'd love to see it."

"Okay, Babe, if you really want to. We have nothing to lose by looking."

~

We closed the deal two weeks later in mid-July, hardly able to believe our good fortune.

"It's what we call a distressed sale," the real estate agent said. "The previous owners were under pressure to sell in a hurry. Too bad, after they did all those electrical and plumbing renovations."

By the end of the month we had the old, one-time farmhouse cleaned up and ready to move in. Our used and hand-me-down furnishings seemed ready made for the staunch old relic with its worn, wide pine-board floors and high ceilings.

The spacious kitchen with its huge walk-in pantry was our favorite room, the room where we spent most of our time, reading, talking, drinking tea or wine and taking meals, unless we were outside on one of the two wide sitting porches or asleep in one of the four bedrooms. We could hardly keep the smiles off our faces from the sheer and constant pleasure our dream fulfilled had brought.

The dirt road that led from the busy highway to our newly acquired haven passed through several acres of undeveloped woodland before emerging into what had once been the working barnyard. Only a stone and concrete silo remained where the cattle barn, the chicken coup and the machinery shed had stood.

Between the derelict barnyard and the rambling, gray clapboarded house a fenced garden was loaded with un-harvested produce—sweet corn, beans, tomatoes, peppers, okra, squash—our inheritance from the previous owners that we had never met.

On the far side of the house stood the orchard of gnarled, antique peach trees, each still bearing fruit but for the largest of them, a single, sturdy O'Henry standing tall and surrounded by half a dozen Summer Ladies, its branches wide spread but barren.

"Odd, that big old tree has no fruit. It looks as healthy as the rest."

~

We had our first visitors in September, well after the peach harvest, an old couple with the names of Benjamin and Julia Smith. An odd couple they were—she a large, loud woman with a ready laugh, he a wiry imp of a man who spoke with the hint of a British accent and had the devil's twinkle in his eye. They told us they were our nearest neighbors from the other side of the woods. We chatted over cups of strong and fragrant Earl Grey tea at our kitchen table.

"Hope you folks decide to stay. Seems like someone just moves into this old place and they're moved out again."

"We can assure you that we plan to stay. We love it here. It's our dream house."

We showed the Smiths around the place, though they seemed disinterested, as if already familiar with it, more familiar than ourselves. We showed off the new swing we had hung that week on the wide back porch, and from there we wandered into the orchard. The trees that had given us their abundant harvest now pointed their barren branches toward the gray, autumn sky.

"We had a great peach crop this year, except for that one tree. Next year we will bring you some."

"Don't you know about that tree? That is where they hanged the scoundrel, McComber, after he killed his darling young wife. Way back when these trees were young. Strangest thing. They say that tree never bore fruit since."

As the old couple took their leave, we bade them safe travel and invited them to return soon. "Don't stay away, now that you know we are here. We'd love to hear more of your eerie tales."

~

Cool autumn breezes scattered the withered peach tree leaves along the fence of the dormant garden. The nights turned cold. We enjoyed our first crackling wood fire in the old stone fireplace. I wondered if she heard the voices too.

The steaming bowls of porridge looked and smelled inviting. Just the thing for a cold, late-October morning. Later, we would carve the Jack O'Lanterns, fit them with fat candles and set them out on the front porch. It was our usual Halloween ritual, although, in our new remote location, visitors begging for treats would be unlikely. For the present, we both enjoyed the warming, filling, rare treat of porridge.

Finished, I fixed our coffees, hers black, mine creamed and sugared. She took a grateful sip and said, "I didn't hear you up early making porridge. What made you think of that? We never have porridge. But it was great."

"Are you being coy? I don't know porridge from a pothole. And I sure didn't get up early."

Her face reddened. "Don't tease me. It's not funny. Someone made the porridge."

"But . . . I swear, I . . . ."

"Not Funny!"

Later that morning, while we were still not speaking, Benjamin and Julia stopped by for a friendly visit. "Hope we're not imposing by coming unannounced. We often roam about on Halloween."

We almost forgot the porridge incident as we sipped our tea and talked about the change in the weather and such. Eventually, I asked, "About this McComber, how did he kill his wife?"

"Poisoned her, they said. Put strychnine in her morning porridge, they said, and went out to the barn to do the morning milking. Her kinfolks came by and found the fair young bride stretched out dead, with a horrible grimace on her beautiful face. Still warm. Right here, on this very kitchen floor. They found the foul McComber in the barn, hauled him out, all fussing and protesting, and hanged him from that old peach tree. All the while, him shouting and screaming his innocence."

We heard the voices now more clearly and more often. Young voices. Happy voices, speaking of love, speaking of the future. Then a woman's raucous laughter ended abruptly. The script varied but little. Then a sad, profound silence filled the old house.

And every morning, steaming bowls of porridge that we dared not eat.

~

We packed the last of our things into our overloaded van and locked the back door. A fine white blanket of snow had been deposited the night before. Stubbles and stalks in the dormant garden stood above the cold dusting as if to wish us a forlorn farewell. We drove slowly, without speaking, past the *For Sale* sign at the edge of the lawn. As I turned to look upon the deserted silo one last time, the semblance of foot prints appeared in the snow, like someone being dragged toward the vacant old house.

I sped toward the woods.

"I wonder what Benjamin and Julia will think. We told them that we would never leave."

"We have never visited their place. We'll just stop to say goodbye. To let them know we are leaving. Do we dare tell them why?"

We searched for the mailbox number the Smith's had given us. Finding it, we pulled into the long driveway.

Ahead, the tower of a fine old Victorian rose above the trees. The stained and mottled gingerbread had once been painted bright cream, in contrast with the dark mauve of the shingled siding. Children's toys and bicycles lay abandoned on the broad, somewhat neglected front lawn.

We rang the doorbell, and heard voices from within. A man and woman, younger than ourselves, smiled and greeted us. Children laughed with delight in another room. The woman turned briefly and called out, "Peter, Priscilla. Not so loud!" and returned her attention to us.

"Hello. We just stopped to say goodbye to Benjamin and Julia."

"Benjamin? Julia?"

"Yes. The Smiths."

"Oh?" The young husband glanced at his wife, then back at us. He frowned. "There was a couple named Smith that lived here." He cracked a wry smile. "About a century ago. Not now."

"But, we saw them just a few weeks ago. At the old McComber place."

The woman stepped forward. "Sorry. I am certain that the Smiths we have any knowledge of, Benjamin and Julia, died many years ago. Executed, if you want the truth. This was their home, we were told."

She raised a hand to her throat. "It's said that they lynched that man with the name you mentioned . . . uh . . . McComber. They thought he'd killed their daughter. Priscilla was her name. Found out some time later she died of a stroke. Unusual for one so young. Too late for them. Sadly and surely, too late for the poor bloke, McComber. Tragic, all around."

"But. How?" We both uttered quietly. Wide-eyed, not really believing, we took a small step back.

"I say old chap, can you and the missus stay a while?" the man reached out and gripped my arm, though I did not feel his touch. "We would love to have you two join us a while. We were just fixing breakfast. We're having bangers and nice hot homemade porridge. It's an old family recipe."

Richard Allen Anderson

The Attendant

Ida stared into the darkness of her lonely room, listening, waiting. Heavy footsteps of the attendant approached down the nursing home hallway, vacant now of the wheelchaired patients that lined its walls in daylight hours.

The door creaked open. A sliver of pale light spilled across the darkness onto her bed. Lacking visitors from kith or kin, she had come to look forward to the nocturnal visits when they began. But, now.

Shivering, she pulled the covers over her nose and willed her eyes shut, sensing the attendant beside her.

"Good evening, Ida."

She winced at the silky sound of the attendant's voice. She clamped her eyes and mouth shut, hoping to stifle any involuntary whimpers.

"I know you are awake, Ida."

The almost nightly ritual sent tremors through her frail body and made her aging brain reel.

"I see you were naughty today, Ida. You soiled yourself and your bedclothes after lunch."

Her lunch tray had been the usual bland stuff except for Salisbury steak and a special treat that she held now close to her heart.

"You know I must punish you, Ida, for being naughty again. Now roll over."

Punishment was always the same, although the means of applying the whippings to her bare back and buttocks varied. The bruises were rarely detected. If they were, the attendant had ready explanations. And no one really cared.

"Come now, Ida, you know it is easier if you cooperate."

Ida gripped the covers tightly. The voice carried more menace now.

"Guess I will have to roll you over then. That will cost you extra licks."

The attendant pulled the covers away and bent to turn Ida on her stomach.

Ida struck with all the might her failing body could muster. The heavy steak knife the kitchen help had neglected to retrieve that afternoon now plunged through the attendant's flabby neck, ripping the carotid and sending warm blood spurting across the bed. The attendant slumped onto the cold tile floor, without a word, without a whimper.

Ida closed her eyes at last and slept like a baby.

I Can't Remember My Name

She left me here, that red-haired woman. Who was she? Where is she now? I liked her. But I don't like it here.

They leave me alone a lot. Most of the time. That's good. They bring food and drink aplenty. Not all that great. I think I'm getting fat. Eat and sleep. All I do.

Usually have to wake me to eat. That one in the gray dress brings me ice cream in the afternoon too. Caught her a good one a while back when she shook me. They all came fussing at me then. I don't strike out at her anymore. I like ice cream.

She gave me this notebook too. Says to write more in it. She don't have to bother. I can hardly write now. But I can read some. I read in the notebook about the people. I don't know them, but I feel good then—mostly. Some words are hard. I skip them.

~

Most unusual. Frightening too, if you want to know the truth. I feel like such a fool.

Josie, my darling wife, sent the cops out to find me. I was missing all day. She had already checked the places I might have been, the places where I spend a lot of time since I retired a few years ago. The soup kitchen, I help cook there, but only Tuesdays and Thursdays. I drop in at the library often, to read a little poetry or chat with Emily, the librarian. I'm on the board too. They looked for me at the Y, but I don't go there on the weekend. She even had them check Dunkin Donuts. I only go there sometimes early for coffee and a bagel.

They found me in that big park with the lake and geese across town. I was exhausted and happy they found me really. I'd been jogging. She should have known. Block after block, mile after mile, more than usual. Suddenly nothing looked familiar. I kept going, trying to remember how to get home. Then I had to stop and sit and rest.

I watched the sailing skiffs race for about an hour. I watched a few innings of a Little League game. The kids were pretty funny, chasing the ball while the batter ran the bases. I napped on the park bench. Still no clue how to get home. The sun was dropping low. A woman walking a dog asked if I was okay. I told her, Oh yes, just resting. Thank you.

But I was hungry. The air was growing cold. The more I thought about what to do, the more confused I got. So I stayed sitting on the bench while the sun went down.

Josie didn't say much when they brought me into the house. She just looked at me funny and worried-like—and angry too. She told me to wash up, and she put some reheated dinner out for me to eat. It was pot roast and pineapple upside down cake for dessert. It was good to be home. Later in bed, I lay awake for a long time.

Next day, I tried to explain how I just couldn't find my way home. It seemed like the more I tried the farther away I got. I don't think she understood. Neither do I. After that, we didn't talk more about it, and things went along as usual, but I am writing it all down.

~

Josie, that's my wife, keeps real busy. She likes to do things with her hands—painting or knitting or fixing things that get broke. She talks on the phone a lot too, one of our kids or another or maybe a grandchild. I love when the grandchildren visit, but I can't keep all their names straight.

~

After I got lost another time or two, the kids bought me a treadmill and said for me to jog at home in the basement. It's not the same, so I don't use it much. They said not to drive anymore either unless someone was with me. I don't mind that.

~

My activities have been changing, little by little. I don't go out jogging or even walking, and I never go to the Y to work out. I spend a lot of time watching television now. Josie, my wife, picked out shows for me, and I liked what she chose. Nova and National Geographic and that sort of thing. Sometimes, though, it is hard to follow. Sometimes I just fall asleep with the TV running, even during the daytime. Now and then, I pick up this notebook and think about making some notes, like now.

~

That woman, I think she's my wife, doesn't go out unless I come along. We do everything together— shopping, haircuts, lunch at that Italian restaurant we both like. Of course, I don't go anywhere without her or one of the kids. I don't see my friends, hardly at all now.

I try doing things for myself. That seems to upset the woman. She doesn't smile as much as she used to. She scolded me for getting up at night and making a mess in the kitchen and leaving a burner lit on the stove top. She lets me know when to change my clothes or take a shower. Sometimes she has to help. I don't mind that.

~

I hope the kids cannot tell when I don't know their names. I love having them visit. I don't want to hurt their feelings. The boy hurt, though, when I couldn't say his name or even recognize him at first. He told me, It doesn't matter, Dad. Just a Senior Moment. But I knew.

~

The woman is good to me. She told me, Change your clothes now. Underwear and everything. They're all on the bed.

I knew something was up. We drove through town to a big building somewhere. It looked nice with flowers all around in front. The sign on the door said Pleasant Manor or something like that.

We took an elevator up to another floor and sat down to wait. There were magazines, but I didn't bother with them. They don't make much sense to me anymore. I look at the pictures sometimes and pretend that I'm reading.

She took my hand and said, We are going to talk with Doctor Sing now.

I laughed out loud. Doctor Sing!

The doctor didn't look in my throat or ask me to roll up my sleeve. He just talked to me and asked me a lot of questions. He looked at my friend, the woman sitting in the corner, and asked her some questions too. I missed some of the answers.

I couldn't remember what name the month had, but I knew it was warm, so I said Summer. I could tell him we had three children, but I think I screwed up their names. I said there was one boy and two girls. The doctor said that was good.

Then he says, And what is your name?

I had not thought about that for a while. I told him I could not come up with that just then.

He wrote for quite a while on a notepad. After a while he said, Can you tell me who is that red-haired woman sitting in the corner?

No problem, I said, I'm not sure who she is. I think her name is Josie, and I love her.

~

Sometimes I close my eyes, and real clear thoughts come to me. Mostly, I like to think about my pals when I was young. Some of the crazy-fun things we did—car racing, girl chasing, swimming across Fish Lake at midnight. I'm all alone, but sometimes it seems like I can feel that red-haired woman near me, touching me, and she says, What are you grinning about?

Richard Allen Anderson

Minor Differences

Her bare shoulders were warm and inviting under his cold hands. They carried the subtle scent of her favorite perfume, earthy and animal.

"Ohhh. Are you leaving me now?" Her husky whisper was still heavy with sleep. "Don't' leave. Come back in bed with me."

"It's almost eight. I can't be late again." He had showered, shaved and dressed for work and caught two minutes of the Weather Channel and a snatch of the Today Show news and celebrity gossip before returning to the bedroom to waken her.

"I'm all dressed and ready to go," he said. Her hand caught his, pulling him to her. Bending to plant a platonic peck on her cheek, he felt her lazy warmth rise to meet him. She turned her head to receive his lips on hers and reached up to pull his shampooed head down to her searching mouth.

"Baby, I've got to go . . . !"

Later, he considered calling in sick and spending the rest of the morning in bed. But, he was not practiced at deceit, and he deferred to duties beyond his connubial obligations. Quickly redressing in the semi-darkness of the shaded room, he prepared to leave without further contact or goodbyes. She did not lift her face from the pillowed comfort of puffy down to acknowledge or resist his departure except to utter a satisfied, throaty, "Bye now, Mik."

"Bye Nettie," he said, and quickly grabbed the car keys from the dresser.

~

51

At least rush hour is over, he thought, and parked in a far corner of the Universal Engineering office lot. He strode toward the double glass entry doors. His thoughts shifted reluctantly from his early morning activities to the tasks and problems that would confront him during the next eight hours.

Inside, the receptionist absently handed him two pink message slips. Her bottle-black hair hung loosely, covering half of her face as she spoke quietly and confidentially into the telephone. She did not look up or bother to address him by name. He hadn't learned her name either. He called her Gina—of the species Lollobrigida.

She did make an attractive welcome mat to greet visitors, but except for the top brass and a few young studs like Brad, she could not waste any of her limited attention span on most of the staff. Mik's own preference was for brains over boobs, but he doubted any man could help but appreciate her up-front assets.

He glanced at the pink sheets. *Good, the one o'clock meeting is cancelled. No reason given. And Brad is back and wants to talk. Waiting in my office, I suppose.*

He'd hired Brad Stone three years ago to help catch up with checking specifications on the minor engineering drawings that kept piling up. Stone lacked academic credentials, but he was a quick study. Where he lacked raw brain-power, he more than compensated with determination, study and hard work.

He had given Brad personal attention and mentoring to develop his raw potential and had alerted top management to Brad's achievements. And he had come to rely on Brad, gradually delegating more complex and difficult problems to him.

"Hey, old man," Brad greeted him, "you're smiling, and you're late. Catch an early nooner?"

Mik raised an eyebrow and thought, *sometimes you are a little too perceptive.* He dropped his attaché case on his desk, smiled and reached out to shake Brad's hand and throw an arm around his shoulders. "Let's get some coffee, my friend."

Mik had come to regard and treat Brad like the younger brother he never had, and Brad reciprocated with warm respect. Yet something remote and undefined limited their friendly intimacy. Maybe it was the working relationship. Maybe it was the age difference or generation gap. Whatever, it was always there, like a haunting fragrance, perceptible but unidentified.

The office crew had finished with coffee and break-room gossip an hour ago; the dark dregs from the Pyrex pot were strong and bitter. "No time to make fresh, this will have to do," Mik said. "Do you want some of the swill? You seem busting with news. How was your trip?"

"It'll wait till we get back to your office," Brad said. Then, unable to resist his constant exuberance, he whispered, "I'm getting married again, Mik."

Stone had been married two years ago for exactly eight months. Julie, his bride, a beautiful, slim blonde, was a perfect complement to her tall, broad-shouldered, raven-haired husband. They cohabited for a year, before Brad had acquiesced to set the wedding date. Finally they eloped for a solitary but elaborately staged wedding and honeymoon in Hawaii.

Mik and Nettie were invited to the newlyweds' apartment only once, a few months after the wedding. They sat together on a stiffly upholstered settee to view photos of the happy couple in tux and short white wedding dress holding hands and embracing under a canopy of orchids, or tanned and athletic in shorts and tees with a grotto waterfall splashing behind them, or in a mock pose with Brad rescuing a wide-eyed Julie from the rim of a steaming volcano.

They had given up the appropriate responses, a duet of "ohs" and "ahs" and "beautifuls," while leafing through the expensive, professional album, while Brad and Julie sat stiffly together on the settee opposite from them. Each had felt ill-at-ease with the newly-weds, sensing something oddly amiss in the elaborate picture show and something lacking or fictitious in the young couple's current behavior.

On their drive home, Nettie was the first to remark, "God, I felt like I was at a bad Neil Simon play. Like they were pretending . . . posing all the time. They acted so un-newly-married, didn't you think? Maybe it was just the feeling I got from those cold furnishings—they looked like samples from that ultra-modern furniture showroom at the mall."

"I'd say the furniture is a reflection of themselves. Smart, stylish and expensive. But yeah, they were so, uh, perfunctory . . . not at all intimate." Mik dropped his hand on Nettie's thigh. "Not even a pat on the ass. If you treated me like that, I'd think you were hinting at divorce."

Mik and Nettie's furnishings comprised an informal and varied collection of mostly early-American pieces, overstuffed contemporary and inherited or purchased antiques of any era or origination. The collection had grown sporadically over the years, and somehow, it all fit together, a comfortable mélange they both approved.

When Mik proposed marriage, Nettie had said, "We're just too different."

Mik replied, "It'll keep life interesting, you'll see."

Over the years, he had repeated this assertion, always in response to her "We are so different," or "We don't agree on anything."

There was some truth in both of their statements. Differences abounded in their tastes in food, music and literature even after years of marriage. Nettie was strictly meat and potatoes. Mik went for extensive smorgasbords or exotic international cuisine. He detested the hip-hop and rap that turned her on, as much as she disliked the classics or the Coltrane he loved. They disagreed on points of religion, although neither of them practiced one formally or attended any church. They disagreed on politics, but neither were strong members of any party.

Once, in their fifth year of marriage, while their furnishings were more meager but less worn, she had said to him one evening, out of the blue, "Maybe we should get a separation."

The notion was so remote to Mik, it was as if she had spoken a foreign language. The words just did not register. "What?" was all he could manage to respond.

"Nothing. Go back to your reading." And she let the statement recede from her consciousness, like a stone skipping away over quiet water.

In fact, their bond was strong and genuine. Their basic perceptions and values were rarely dissimilar. Motherhood and Apple Pie. Honesty and Integrity, Home and Family and God bless the USA. Both were predisposed to kindness and consideration, not only for each other but for those less fortunate. Both were imbued with a need to care and to share, yet either could tear out your throat or your heart with spiteful slams if aroused in the heat of argument.

Nettie's killer instinct was more highly developed— she had majored in psychology with a minor in American

Lit. She was more likely to hurl the hurtful phrase, then rush back like Florence Nightingale to repair the wounds with skilled understanding and gentle compassion.

Mik, careful and deliberate, eschewed pernicious utterances until he flew over the edge, out of control. Only then did he select the most vicious and cutting articulations of attack. With that release, he withdrew for hours or days of brooding, resentment, and remorse.

Each knew the others soft spots well. They both had learned to avoid them unless willing to suffer the anguish of the retaliation almost sure to follow. Each anticipated the other's thoughts or reactions, whether agreeable or not. Though as comfortable together now as their dissimilar and well-used furniture, each still thought the other to be the most interesting person on the planet. And they were good in bed together.

Neither of them had been surprised when Brad announced that Julie had moved in with another man and was suing for divorce based on irreconcilable differences. Nor did it seem odd that Brad seemed hardly perplexed. He continued his private life as he had before and during the marriage—heavily involved in spectator and participation sports, body training four times a week at Singleton's Spa and pick-up basketball games at the Y.

It seemed to both of them that Brad had undertaken marriage and later dismissed it much as he might have impulsively purchased a stylish new suit or a sporty new car, then quickly tired of it to the point of neglect and eventual abandonment. But they continued to wonder about the true nature of those irreconcilable differences.

~

Walking back to Mik's office, Brad attracted the usual flirtations from female secretaries and receptionists, single and married, young and old. They all appreciated his considerate and deferential good manners but especially his smashing good looks.

Need a favor from one of them? Have Brad Stone ask her for it. He plied them with a wink and a smile, a quick personal inquiry or a bad, bad joke. Stone was not the brightest bulb in the chandelier, but he did have a unique shine

Mik shut the office door. His surprise at Brad's whispered announcement in the break room had abated with the short walk back to his office, like the cooling of the hot, bitter coffee. Still, he was eager to know more. "Okay, let's hear about it," he said.

"Well, the wedding date is two weeks from today—a civil ceremony. We want you and Nettie to be our witnesses. No one else is coming."

"Wow, that was fast!" He refrained from adding, are you sure this time? He said, "I'm not sure what's on our calendar two weeks from now, but it's probably not anything we can't change. Nettie will be very happy for you. You know I am, too."

Mik sat on the edge of his desk, eying the telephone. He itched to call home, to tell Nettie. He thought how he might phrase the surprise announcement and hoped she would not still be in the shower. He realized he still lacked some essential information to pass on.

"So, Brad, who is the lucky girl who will claim you as her prize? You haven't mentioned seeing anyone regularly . . . much less a new love life . . . or that you've been thinking of a new wife."

Brad blinked studiously and cleared his throat. Mik had never known his friend to lack confidence in any situation. Now he watched Brad Stone shift his gaze nervously from the office window to meet his own eyes and back again.

"We've kept it very quiet," Brad said, "and it won't be a new wife for me, it will be a new husband."

Mik's mouth twisted as if he'd just ingested something of doubtful or distasteful origin. He thought, *what the hell are you talking about, man?*

He said, "A new husband? That makes no sense, Brad."

Brad smiled but offered little in the way of explanation. "You may have seen him on televsion sometime. He's the wrestler—The Unholy Terror. Also known as Norman Kramer."

"But, he's a man!" Mik blinked stupidly.

"You got it, boss."

~

Mik stirred the ice and liquor slowly, chilling the Absolute and Martini & Rossi Extra Dry until the flask developed a haze of condensation, the signal to decant.

"Sure you won't have one with me?" he asked. "I need to talk with you about something. It may take a while."

"No thanks, babe. I had a quiet day and I'm pretty mellow already." Nettie opened the oven door, checking the chicken casserole she had prepared for their dinner. It was one of her specialties, and already it smelled delicious.

"Then just come sit with me." Mik strained the cold, clear liquid into a wide-mouthed, long-stemmed martini glass, the kind he reserved for special occasions. "Maybe you'd better turn the oven down to low for a while."

He proceeded between long sips to reveal Brad's news, the wedding plans first and then, fumbling the words, the fact that it would be a homosexual union.

Nettie sat across from Mik, leaning in with her arms on the kitchen table. She seemed to absorb all the information as easily as if he had told her Brad had a dentist appointment or was planning a trip around the world.

"I'm not surprised," she said, "I've always wondered about Brad."

"But he's such a hunk, as you women say."

Nettie patted the back of Mik's hand. "What planet do you live on? They always are!" She rose to check the casserole. "Maybe you should fix me one of your silver bullets, after all."

He made a double batch with fresh ice and a little extra vermouth, the way she liked it, and returned to the table with the two full glasses. "But that's not all. Here's the kicker . . . where it becomes a dilemma for you and me. He wants us to witness the ceremony at city hall. Then he wants us to have dinner with the two of them holding hands and making dove eyes, and see them off on the honeymoon!"

"That is so nice of him to want us there. What's your dilemma? Brad has always had a lot of respect for you. It's wonderful he has enough confidence to ask for your support now."

"That's it? You're not even mildly disturbed, much less appalled or horrified? We are talking about being official guests at, and party to, a gay wedding . . . with Brad as the beautiful bride!"

"I've never heard you talk like this before. Since when are you Mr. Homophobe?"

"Well, this is someone we know!" Mik's guts battled with his brain. "They can do what they want behind closed doors, no matter how repulsive it may be. At least we were not involved in it—until now. I do not like the public displays or acceptance of it . . . it's not natural."

"My God, would you listen to yourself? You've read enough to know it is inborn. It's in his genes, in his blood. It's not a matter of choice. It is natural. Maybe not for us, but for them it is."

"I never bought that. Not 100 percent. Anyway, why do they have to get married? It shouldn't even be allowed. Marriage has always meant a man and a woman."

"Listen, dear," she said, "I am happy and proud to live in this country where homosexual marriage is finally and universally sanctioned and legal." The glass shook in her hand, spilling out a few drops. "Where is your cherished notion of equality without that?"

"The constitution doesn't say anything about gay marriage." He sipped slowly, feeling the booze ease his taut nerves. He knew his statement was hollow and incoherent and felt relieved when Nettie chose not to challenge it.

"Brad is practically your best friend ever. How can you condemn him for this? You should be happy he is out of the closet and free to be himself."

"I'm not condemning him. I just do not understand how he can choose that kind of relationship. God, I cannot stand to even think about it."

"I don't really understand either, but sexual orientation is not a matter of choice. At any rate, it's not for us to approve or not. Think of how many have lived in a hell of heterosexual relationships when their natural inclination was homosexual. Think of Brad and Julie. They were miserable together. Why should gays and lesbians have to feign our kind of life to satisfy us? Why should they have to live in clandestine affairs or in solitude?"

"Well, I'd rather they just shut up about it then."

He had read all the opinions on homosexual tendencies and the rights of all Americans, all humans, to enjoy the benefits of a marriage relationship. He had no formal religious beliefs on which to base his objections as others did, citing obscure biblical passages. He just did not like the idea.

"I don't want them flaunting their lifestyle at me. I don't need to see any more Gay Pride parades! God, I suppose Brad and his new husband could be the frigging king and queen in the next one."

The oven beeped and Nettie rose to extract their dinner. "Set the table for me, honey, while I fix a salad and get this casserole ready to serve. And relax, for heaven's sake. You're all flushed."

Their dinner conversation turned to the recent hurricanes in Florida and snippets of local news Nettie had caught on television earlier in the day when she wasn't working on her poetry collection. Then it was quiet, so quiet Mik could hear Nettie's breathing and the tic-toc of the pendulum clock in the hall, each of them reluctant to continue with the subject that remained fixed in both of their minds.

Nettie smiled and broke the silence. "What should we get them for a wedding gift?"

"Jeez. I have no clue what to give a couple of gays."

"Don't think of it in that context."

"How can you not?"

Mik knew he could never see Brad with the same eyes again. Would they ever again be able to shake hands or bear hug as they were accustomed to do?

He watched Nettie's delicate hand holding her dinner fork, absently playing with the food on her plate. He loved her fine hands, her rounded arms, shoulders and neck. He loved the touch of her velvet skin. He loved her delicate face, framed in short-cropped hair that accentuated her femininity and appeal. He loved her shining eyes and her soft lips. The soft curves and the round fullness in her knit cotton blouse urged him to reach out, to feel her close to him.

How could Brad disdain such feminine charms for the arms of a man?

Shadows flickered briefly across Nettie's serious, thoughtful face—shadows of candlelight from the four tapers she had lighted to enhance their dinner and shadows of doubt and concern.

"What did you say to him?" she asked. Her voice was controlled and quiet. "Did you congratulate him, tell him you couldn't wait to meet his fiancé?"

Mik grunted and thought, *Are you kidding?*

He said, "I told him we might have travel plans for that week. We'd have to see if they could be changed."

"So you lied, and you are actually thinking of abandoning him."

"What else could I do? God, he knocked me over with this whole idea."

"Isn't he the same Brad you have loved dearly for the past three years?"

"The same Brad?" Mik exploded. "Hell no! He's about to become someone's blushing bride for God's sake. A wrestler's bride! Mrs., uh . . . Mrs. Norman Kramer." His last words trailed off. "He will never be Brad Stone again to me . . . ."

Nettie stared at her husband. "How sad," she whispered and pushed back her chair. She rose and moved deliberately around the table to Mik's side. "Get up," she said, and he obeyed, facing her. She looked up into his confused face and ran her smooth fingers up his arms. She grasped him tightly like an unruly child.

"Tomorrow you will tell him we will be honored and delighted to stand by him at his wedding. Tomorrow you will ask if he can bring Norman to our house for dinner next week so we can meet him and get to know him a little before the wedding. Tomorrow you will tell him we will continue to stand by them while other friends and acquaintances abandon them and shun them, for surely that will happen. Brad knows that. Our government recognizes the legality and value of their relationship, but most of the people he knows won't accept them any more. They will be talked about and treated like some kind of dirty joke."

She released her grip. "And you'd better hope he still accepts you."

She paused. "I wonder if they plan on having a family."

Nettie's touch and clear instructions had calmed him, but Mik's longstanding and deeply rooted sentiments persisted. "They're two men, Nettie. They can't have kids. If they could, how would the child feel, having a couple of gays for parents?"

"I know two lesbian couples from the tennis club," she said and stood back with folded arms. "One has kids."

"Two more couples! Christ, it's getting epidemic. You never mentioned them before."

Richard Allen Anderson

"It never came up. Anyway, they are both loving couples and seem quite normal—if there is such a thing—in every other way. One couple—Cindy and Mary—have adopted two kids. One boy and one girl. They are so proud of them. They talk about them all the time, just like other parents. They dress the kids well. They love them. They have the same concerns and worries and aspirations as any other parent . . . and then some."

"But the kids can't feel good about it," he said over his shoulder as he carried dinner dishes to the dishwasher.

Nettie followed and turned him to face her. "You're transferring your own feelings to them. I've met them. The kids are like any others I know except they know they have two moms. Makes them feel special. They accept it without question."

"But they'll be influenced to think a homosexual relationship is normal."

"All I know is those kids are some of the best adjusted and best behaved I've ever met, the most knowledgeable for their age, the most aware. The moms have told me they do not want to predispose the children to homosexuality or heterosexuality. Quite the opposite."

Now she was flushed. She held Mik's face in her two hands. "Damn it, don't you know that after their own struggles with sexual preference, they don't want the kids to face the trauma or the social stigma that homosexuality carries. That will be with us for years to come. Maybe forever. Don't you see, they just want the kids to be very aware . . . to help them make their own choices . . . and to understand the consequences."

Her voice rose as emotions flooded her words. "They should not be second class citizens any longer." Then, looking at Mik's pinched lips between her fingertips, she laughed. Her grip on his face had tightened, making him look like the grill of an Edsel. "Didn't mean to get on a rant," she said and dropped her hands.

Mik looked at her uncertainly, wondering where this all might end for them, for Brad, for society.

She kissed his bewildered face on the cheek and said, "Sorry."

Mik pulled her close and folded her in his arms. Thus they stood for several moments in quiet, domestic embrace, holding on to themselves, holding on to each other.

"I love you."

"I love you too."

Richard Allen Anderson

Yesterday's Rain

Raindrops fell from the barren branches of the gnarled oak tree. That was yesterday.

Today, we summon our small energies and celebrate, eating one hard, dried trout from our meager cache, washed down with careful, grateful swallows of the heavenly gift of water. Until yesterday, there had been no rain for twenty nine months.

The landscape, once lush and verdant with sweet gum, oak, maple and pine has withered to brown and gray from the manmade drought. Joyous clouds of springtime dogwood blooms, splashes of bright azaleas and glorious rhododendrons ceased to appear long ago and will not be seen again. Trees and shrubs had bravely resisted the pernicious radiation from sterile clouds that circled the globe, until their parched roots gradually shriveled and died. Died searching for moisture in the hard red clay.

Marauding hordes of hungry human predators stripped the fields of standing crops during the first year of the holocaust. They left nothing but chaff and dross to feed the roaming herds of domestic or displaced wild animals.

Those contaminated carcasses then too were devoured by the dwindling remnants of humanity. Bleached, white bones, human and animal alike, litter the plains, baking in the unrelenting sun.

All of civilization is gone. We subsist in the wild, like our ancient ancestors, on roots and nuts and small fish scooped from the shallow, putrid remnants of lakes and streams.

We do not know who started the war, who prevailed, who survived—or if others like us are postponing death in isolation for one reason alone: that our infant child might grow to independence.

Our child, Hope, sits laughing against the trunk of the sad oak tree. Yesterday's rain, the first of her experience, delighted her. She curiously strokes the soft green sprouts that have burst forth from the moistened earth, as she stares with unsighted eyes toward the clear blue sky.

The ghosts of ancient civilizations carry with them secrets that modern archeologists and anthropologists attempt to unravel from the interred accouterments and bones of the long dead. It has long been believed the ghosts that inhabit the remote island of Tristan da Cuhna are younger than ghosts anywhere else on the planet Earth. But the ghosts one might encounter, should one somehow come to these desolate shores, may be more reclusive and obscure than the ghosts of England or even America where at least some of their living souls originated.

The ghost of one particular soul who once found refuge in the relatively recent island settlement, called Edinburgh of the Seven Seas, is shrouded in mystery and invokes intense curiosity in all who learn of it. We have come to know of this ghost, not from exhumed bones, but through a small volume known today as Davidson's Notebook.

~

Near the time the first pre-humans were descending from trees to stand upright and walk on the African savannah, molten magma from deep in the earth's mantle pushed upward from a giant crack in the ocean floor 1700 miles west of the South African coast.

By the time the first of the species homo sapiens evolved, three million years later, the volcanic cone had risen more than three fourths of a mile above the mid-Atlantic fissure to protrude above the ocean waves. Yet another 200,000 years would elapse before Portuguese explorer, Tristoa da Cunha, sailed upon the uncharted island. Its dark cliffs rose 2000 feet above the sea and the igneous rock mass spanned more than seven miles across. While human diaspora had long populated every continent on earth by the year of da Cunha's discovery in 1506, no species of the Homo genus had reached this remote and uninviting place—at least, so it was thought.

The nearest land occupied by humans was many hundreds of miles distant. Parasitic eruptions on the active volcano's slopes continued to add fresh lava flows and poison the atmosphere. Strong winds buffeted the rugged cliffs. Rain fell from dark, cloudy skies on two days out of three. Yet, over the next four centuries, Tristan da Cuhna, the most isolated place on earth, acquired a small farming community of European and American settlers who occupied the island's northwestern shore. What brought them to this uninviting place? What is their story?

~

In 1961, a new volcanic eruption split the earth adjacent to the tiny town of Edinburgh of the Seven Seas, aka The Settlement, threatening homes and lives and causing the evacuation of all 280 of Tristan's inhabitants. All, that is, but one.

The remarkable and mysterious adventure of Franklin Davidson is known to us only from the contents of the torn and blood-stained notebook discovered in the small cottage that was once home to Davidson, his wife, Edna and two young daughters when the displaced settlers returned to the island in 1963. (1)

~

November 12. I am alone.

My heart beat as cold and black as the forbidding cliffs of this lonely island while the ships carried my dear family, my friends and neighbors out to sea and beyond the horizon. No other ships will sail within sight for months, even years. Can I endure this bruising isolation?

Edna, Violet and Sienna will be in Cape Town by now. From there they will find ultimate refuge in England with the rest of our neighbors from this place. But I cannot risk a return to the other civilization that once welcomed me.

I cannot risk being identified. I cannot tolerate a return to prison. Perhaps, by now, the authorities have discovered my absence. They will not return to rescue one lone occupant of this endangered and now desolate place— unoccupied but for the dogs, the cows and sheep, the penguins, and me. (2)

December 12.

I have heard no human voice nor felt no human touch for a month. Yet I sense somehow I am not alone. The cinder cone has grown almost daily with fresh eruptions, erratic spewing from the bowels of the earth. Lava flows out into the sea but, thus far, remains outside of town while hot cinders and ash fly in all directions. I cannot venture out without my heavy boots and jacket in spite of the rising temperatures. Some days, I must remain inside or choke on the oppressive sulfurous atmosphere.

The loneliness is more oppressive still, though I have endured separation before. Will I ever see my family again?

December 25. Christmas.

I placed fresh holly sprigs on the mantle and lighted a candle on the table, hoping to feel some of the warmth and joy of this springtime holy day. My spirit has not been cheered.

During the long and lonesome daytimes, I occupy myself with tending the livestock that was left behind, late spring plowing and planting and harvesting the last few winter potatoes from the fields. Many family pets were abandoned in the evacuation, and I feed and water those cats and dogs that find our door. And I have buried some others.

At night, I read by the light of my kerosene lantern, as the generators no longer run. I have borrowed books and other items from the neighbors' houses. I doubt they will mind. One lonely night, I slept in the Jackson's bed rather than return to mine.

January 15. Midsummer.

The snow is gone from Queen Mary's Peak. Hot lava, just yards away from our homes, has raised the air temperature noticeably above our accustomed summer highs of 70 degrees. Lava creeping into the sea sends up clouds of steam and noxious fumes. When will this abate? When will it be safe for my family to return? Even the gulls have abandoned this place.

January 21.

Yesterday, the new volcano threw hot rocks this way. The home on the edge of town was struck and burned to the ground. Fear and foreboding have intruded on my mind. I must think of abandoning The Settlement and our now desolate home until the eruptions abate.

February 1.

The earth growls and rumbles beneath my feet. Night or day, I know not when to forecast it coming. I have loaded a rucksack and gunny sack with clothing, ropes and tackle, canned goods and potatoes. It is as much as I can carry, and might provide sustenance for many weeks if I am careful. The small flask of Jameson's may help cheer my journey.

February 5.

The rain is cold on my face today. A hint of winter already? I am proceeding south, through Runaway Beach and the potato patches toward The Bluff. Beyond this, my route is uncertain as the cliffs will obstruct my progress.

I will attempt a climb into one of the deep gulches, following it into the unexplored interior. I have provided just sufficient feed for the dogs and livestock to fend for themselves until I return in a few weeks' time.

February 10.

I fired three shots today, only to break the quietness. That frightened off some of the nesting birds, the only living creatures sharing this small island with me.

Species that are not common to The Settlement abound here in the interior while the familiar seabirds are rare. A variety of small songbirds, some in colorful hues and others in dull grays and browns. They rarely sing as autumn approaches, so as not to alert the smallish hawks that make their meals of songbirds, plucking them from the air or as they perch, unaware, on the top branches of a rare shrub. The hawks prey too on the occasional errant gull drafting on the sea breeze rising over the cliffs. One fat gull is worth ten of the songbirds.

I carry my revolver, though I have found nothing on this vacant island to hunt or fear. Still, somehow, I feel another presence. Vegetation is sparse, in spite of the copious rainfall, mostly low, spindly shrubs that sometimes sport cheerful blooms of red or yellow or blue.

The winds howling and whistling many days carry faint, familiar smells of the living seas to my eager nostrils, but away from the sound of the sea crashing on the shore, the interior surrounds me, quiet as death except for the occasional cheerful chirping or terrified twitters of a songbird. Not even the low moan of a distant ship passing in the fog.

I have had my meager dinner. Now, I must sleep.

March 3.

My clothing is torn and my hands are raw and bloodied from climbing on the rough, rocky surfaces most of the interior comprises. It has become necessary to ration my food supplies, as this exploration is consuming more time than I anticipated. I persist in my explorations in spite of the hardships. Here is purpose and challenge and adventure. What else do I live for?

I deem one small meal each day may be sufficient to maintain adequate strength for this strenuous trek but little beyond that. I have found edible berries on small bushes growing out of rock fissures. I do not know these berries, but they seem to cause no harm, fill my belly and help me sleep at night. I am tempted to try songbird meat but doubt I can catch one.

March 12. Edna's birthday.

My thoughts today dwell on my brave, darling wife. I wonder, will she think of me?

She alone stood by me after my wrongful conviction. She alone abetted my escape. She has filled my life these past 18 years. She and the girls. I have nothing without them.

I attempt to stay close to the cliffs, keeping the distant sea in view to maintain my orientation. I estimate I am now near the southernmost end of our island. There is little more to note except more stunted, unfamiliar plants and numerous small caves in the face of the mountain. I am thankful for the berries to supplement my dwindling food supplies. I seem to be losing strength and weight. Yet, I do not wish to turn back before seeing more of this extraordinary place.

March 18.

I saw Sienna and Violet last night. They reached out to me to save me from a delirious dream filled with demons and ferocious dragons. I felt the girls' gentle touch, saw their smiles and heard their words of encouragement. "We love you, dear Dad. Soon we will be together again." I awoke, drenched in cold sweat, and puked.

April 1. Fool's Day.

I have seen them, and I think they have seen me.

April 6.

Small beings, no bigger than the Rock Hoppers. Indeed, I thought at first sight they were penguins, as many of them adorn themselves with plumage. Some cover themselves completely with Rock Hopper hides with feathers intact. And they hop amongst the rocks, like the penguins.

They are not penguins. I think they are humans. Miniature humans. Yes, they are some form of human. As sure as my name is Franklin Robert Davidson.

May 20. I have escaped.

My strength is nearly gone. I must rest most of each day, so progress is slow. My mind has become clouded, like the dreary vapors that engulf this god-forsaken place, but I am bursting with searing memories of this incredible adventure. I struggle for clarity for I fear I may not live to tell any of my kind about my capture and imprisonment by the Penguin People.

I must record the happenings of these past weeks, but now I must sleep.

May 21.

I have no supplies remaining other than this notebook, two small tins of whitefish, one of fruit and my revolver. All of these are foreign to the Penguin People and none is of any value to them. Still, I am convinced that a few of their number follow me now, always stealthy and attempting to remain just out of my sight. Yet I know they are there. Do they mean to assure my safe return home or do they have some other purpose?

As I write, my hands shake from fatigue and from the cold. With winter approaching, the wind at this high elevation is more icy than death, though this does not seem to affect the P.P. They seem to endure the rain and snow without discomfort. Are they immune to pain? I sit protected in the lee of the big rocks, hopeful to complete my journal entries. While I can.

I write from memory.

At first, I observed the little people at a far distance through my binoculars as they retrieved a large seabird from some sort of netting snare. I could not believe what I immediately sensed was true. As I moved closer to observe their habits in detail, they became aware of me but displayed little reaction of fear or surprise. Did they already know of us, of The Settlement?

As to my capture, I was most reluctant to desist from my observations of the P.P. and ventured closer to their habitat. It was then I stumbled into and became ensnared in one of their large bird nets. Before I could free myself, a dozen or more of their number bound me with strong, fine ropes and dragged me, like a living Gulliver, into one of their caves.

Seeing me, the group gathered there became quite agitated, their tiny human faces displaying deep frowns and gaping mouths but not anger. Excited murmurs passed among them, perhaps speculation on what to do with their captive prize.

Many more gathered in the voluminous cavern where I remained on display. They became loudly vocal with squeaking interchanges of varying tone and duration, more animal than human. Still, their demeanor spoke more of curiosity and amazement than of menace.

No one was more amazed than I, and I wondered if I might not soon awake from this dream.

Two leaders, distinguished by stone pendants on threads around their necks, prodded me gently with thin rods as if to be sure I was real flesh and bone or possibly measuring how many meals I might provide. That must have disappointed, as my limbs were now thin and scrawny, my ribs protruding around my swollen abdomen.

My face, reflected in small pools on the cave floor, with shaggy, greying beard and sunken eyes would have frightened my family and my countrymen, though perhaps not this curious and excited throng. The leaders directed some of their members to attend the several wounds I suffered from being dragged across the sharp rocks. They did so with a malodorous green salve. Within the hour, my wounds were healed!

The next day, their agitation due to my presence had diminished, and they now seemed more concerned about my welfare and comfort. I accepted their offerings of fresh water but rejected the proffered raw lobster and krill.

Observing my convulsive shivering, they brought woven mats to cover me. I observed that all members of their community acted with a high degree of kindness and cooperation not often found in my own race. They do not seem to pair, but often act together in groups of three, four or five. Strength in numbers compensate for their diminutive size.

On the third day, feeling my strength near an end, I accepted the lobster, offered on the point of a long stick, and managed to eat without regurgitating.

Then, I spoke, hearing my own voice for the first time in weeks. "Bring me that," and I pointed to my rucksack of rations.

Clearly frightened by the sound of my voice, three brave little persons fetched the sack and laid it cautiously within my reach. I opened two tins and, to their wide-eyed amazement, gratefully gulped down the last tin of sardines with a dessert of peach preserves.

During the weeks of confinement that followed, I determined to take careful mental notes, lest I were to come to doubt the reality of this bizarre situation. Their bodies are sturdy, compact and diminutive, weighing no more, I judge, than 25 pounds and standing no more than 20 inches tall.

Is this an adaptation to accommodate cold? The males cannot be distinguished from females nor can I distinguish variations in age. I have not observed what might be young children in their population. Perhaps their young, who must be puny and vulnerable indeed, are sheltered and hidden in a secret rookery until adolescence or adulthood.

Their number is no more than a few hundred. They take shelter in deep caves above the steep cliffs that drop to the sea. Within the caves, I came to know, they have constructed a labyrinth of tunnels sufficient for all to take shelter.

They have fire that is perpetually attended, used more for light than for heat. They have tools. They are adept at spinning fine, strong yarns and ropes, though I have not discovered the source of the fiber they use, whether animal or vegetable.

Their society and their language are primitive. They have leaders and followers and communicate among themselves with oddly articulated words and by gestures, not dissimilar from the Rock Hopper penguins. Their facial expressions are few. They do not smile.

They subsist primarily on lobster obtained from the sea by divers who descend via the gulches to the narrow beaches, always near nightfall after some mumbo-jumbo ritual around the fire. This occurs no more than once each five days even if food supplies are short.

The number five seems to hold some significance for them. Some wear stone tokens suspended on strings about their necks. The curious tokens bear five small depressions arranged in a circle.

I have seen the same arrangement, along with four other abstract symbols I cannot decipher, displayed on the walls of the cavern and passages that lead to deep caves. Otherwise, they do not seem to have developed a written means of communication.

They set bird traps—nets created from their spun yarns—and sometimes dine on roasted sea birds, though the lobster is eaten raw. Like the Rock Hoppers, they also consume large amounts of krill and fish, but only when lobster is not plentiful.

The little people, as I have come to think of them, also supplement their diet of fish and fowl with lichens, several varieties of berries and the few grains growing sparsely on the highest slopes. Though the Rock Hoppers would be easy prey, they are never hunted for meat.

In the first days that followed my capture and detainment, I attempted communications with their cautious leaders, using sign language and carefully pronouncing words like *berry* and *potato*, or *man* or *free*. This was to no avail, although these were, without doubt, intelligent beings. Was this to be how my adventure ended, bound, weak, helpless and alone?

Confined as I was and in full view, there was no choice but to relieve myself in their presence, much to their amazement and more to their obvious dismay. It may have been this act more than anything else that convinced them that keeping this alien creature in their midst was a mistake. But, would they dispose of the menace or set it free?

At their leaders' direction, they hung a stone amulet around my neck, loosened my bonds and set five or six sentries around me to voice an alarm should I decide to leave. Did that mean they claimed me as their property but would not inhibit my departure?

The sentries' presence was no significant deterrent, yet I remained, hungry to learn more of this unknown race of humans. Weak and near delirium, but torn by curiosity, I remained weeks longer in order to observe their comings and goings, after accommodating my diet to raw lobster and berries.

At last, I feared further delay of returning to The Settlement would be fatally hazardous. When I observed snow falling across the mouth the cave, my escape consisted of merely gathering my few remaining supplies, crawling through the cave's opening and walking away.

This lengthy exposition has sapped my mind and my strength. I must pause.

May 23

I know now I will not survive my return journey. The specter of death is my only companion. I will not see again the humble house that Edna and I and the girls knew as home.

I have devoured the last of my rations. Deathly cold has chilled me through and through. Even the hawks do not fly, but strut and search for food in the rocky crevices where the song birds spend their winter hibernating. The few remaining berries are frozen hard. I have no other food to sustain me.

Weak as a babe, I stumble and fall on these jagged surfaces. My vision is blurred. I yearn only to rest and be warm, to be quiet and end this suffering. My cough brings warm blood to my lips that I eagerly lick and swallow.

Here Davidson's journal ends.

How did Davidson's notebook find its way to where it was discovered? Did he return unharmed with it to Edinburgh of the Seven Seas after all? If so, what became of him? (3) There were provisions enough in the village for an individual to survive for many years. Yet no trace of the man was ever found.

Did curious beings follow him and return his pages of strange markings to its resting place in The Settlement after he met with some mishap?

Were the Penguin People truly benign? Why had their existence never been detected? Did they truly exist outside of the delusions of a man weary of isolation or deranged by hunger? Did their colony die out because they lost the ability to procreate? Were they eradicated by eruptions that poured lava into caves on the southern slopes? Did they leave the island to be discovered again one day at yet another remote and isolated location?

No artifacts or other evidence of the Penguin People have been found by several expeditions that have explored Tristan da Cunha since 1963. Davidson's notebook and the small round stone with five indented markings found with it are, to this day, the only clues to the existence of the lost race of Penguin People.

Author's Notes:

(1) Official records state only that all of Tristan da Cunha's residents were evacuated by boat during the 1961 eruptions.

(2) The farming community of Edinburgh of the Seven Seas raised a variety of livestock including, besides those mentioned by Davidson, notably chickens, geese, ducks,

swine and goats. Potatoes were grown almost exclusively as a subsistence crop.

(3) Davidson's family was not among those who returned to the island in 1963. The search for evidence of his existence or demise was not pursued with vigor by those who were occupied with reestablishing their lives and community on the lonely island.

(4) Davidson probably began his climb into the interior via Third Gulch and proceeded over rugged terrain to the vicinity of Round Hill or Cave Gulch. (See map.)

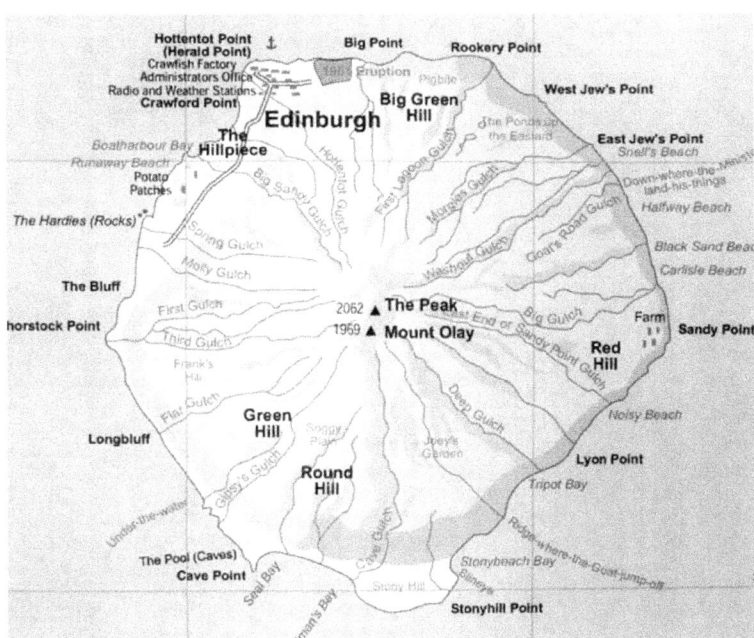

The Island of Tristan da Cunha (4)

Richard Allen Anderson

Mama's Boy

Jim Masters felt good, really good.

"Hey, Rug Rats!" He grinned and waved through the cracked windshield of his aged and rusted pickup. Two little faces laughed and smiled at him from the rear window of a school bus. Children were not offended by the irregular stained teeth that filled his broad smile. They didn't find anything menacing about him.

Children liked Jim instinctively. They often smiled at him in passing, even instigated small conversations. Not so with adults. Although his deeply lined face appeared open and cheerful to a casual glance, up close and friendly he triggered a sense of coldness, even menace. Maybe it was the eyes, shaded under the frayed bill of his sweat-stained baseball cap. Maybe they found the pain they saw deep within too much to tolerate.

The bus turned off, but Jim continued, smiling, flooded with a sense of relief and imbued with a peaceful solitude. He drove with no real destination in mind, somewhere in the suburbs of the city. He had not been aware of his exact location until the approaching intersection stirred some vague recognition—an Eastern Collateral Bank, a Sammy's Pizza, a small strip mall and the red, white and blue badges warning that the interstate was near.

He felt a sudden compulsion to escape this scene. He jammed the wheel to the right, ignoring the blaring of horns and the screeching of brakes around him, and hit the on-ramp doing 50. His smile and his inner tranquility were gone—pushed suddenly and brutally aside.

~

Masters was unmarried and unattached, a loner since childhood. On his tenth birthday his mother walked out on him and his father. His father followed suit six years later, and Jim had not heard of them or from them since.

The Marines had taught him how to fight and kill until they found he had lied about his age and drummed him out. Now, the rare people in his life didn't get close to him. Men ignored him or disdained him. The women, prostitutes or desperate one-nighters, never saw him twice.

As a young student Jimmy Masters fought frustration and endured the ridicule of his classmates. His bright, intuitive child's mind was no match for the "book learning" his schools demanded. No rescuer, no teacher, parent or friend, reached out to share his lonely battle.

~

Jimmy held the schoolbook out towards his mother and pleaded, "Mom, I don't get this."

"Read the book again, Jimmy. It'll come to you."

"Mom, I really don't get it!"

"Damn it, Jim! Would you stop! Don't you see I am busy with my hair and nails?"

Nora Masters watched her small son shuffle from the room. She knew he would not cry and almost laughed with relief when she heard the book slam against the wall and thud to the floor. For a moment before she turned back to the vanity mirror, she felt a twinge of regret. *Little shit. He'll get over it. He'll be fine.*

She watched the woman in the mirror brush her shoulder-length auburn hair and expertly apply eye shadow and bright red lipstick. Satisfied at last, she rose and quickly turned to her closet to select which dress she would wear for her date that night.

Can't still be here when Mory gets home, she thought.

Jimmy sat at the kitchen table, staring at the book page until it blurred and finally went blank. He watched his mother brush into the room. He pretended to read until she nudged his shoulder and handed him a scribbled note. *Heat up the tuna casserole in the fridge for supper when your father comes home. I will be out late.*

"Now you've got my note, Jimmy. No excuse to forget."

Even before the note, her brightly flowered dress and painted face had told him she would be leaving, leaving him alone again. "Mama, please." He rose to embrace her, hoping desperately she might, this once, change her mind and stay.

Nora Masters pushed her son away. "Jimmy, don't. You'll mess me up with your huggin' and kissin'. Now do your homework." She hurried to the door and left without a backward glance.

Alone, Jimmy pulled the dish of leftovers from the refrigerator and emptied its contents on the kitchen floor. He dropped his mother's note onto the mess and mashed it with his foot. He left a trail of tuna footprints leading to his bedroom. By the time his father returned, drunk or sober, he hoped to be asleep. Only in sleep would the pain leave him.

"Fuck you," he said, "fuck you," and punched the pillow as hot tears fell from his eyes. "Fuck you. Fuck you!"

~

Nora didn't bother with a note when she finally left Jimmy and Morris for the pleasure of another man. What could she say, really? For all her dreams of glamour, life with them was just too mundane to bear.

When Nora did not come home one morning, Jimmy pounded and shook his unresponsive father, demanding, "Where's Mama?"

"Damned if I know or care," his father replied, not bothering to look at his son.

After the third day of her absence neither father nor son spoke of her again.

~

Morris Masters was a small man in almost every way. He worked second shift at the factory after graduating from high school and rarely encountered the office staff. He had worked there almost two years when he first met Nora Hembein, the new clerk in accounts and records, when he stopped by the office with a question about his Labor Day overtime pay. She treated him as coldly as yesterday's gravy, and he determined at once to date her. *Hell, I'm gonna marry her.*

He confided to Hank, his one good buddy. "I am going to ask Nora out—you know, the looker in the office."

Hank laughed at him. "She's out every night with a different guy. You ain't got . . . "

"You'll see. Bet you a sawbuck."

Three weeks later, Hank forked over a ten spot to a grinning Morris Masters and listened to his tale of triumph.

"I spent half a week's pay for tickets to see Led Zeppelin, that new rock band. Seemed like she was about to laugh in my face until I showed her the tickets—front row, center!"

After the concert, still aglow with images of Jimmy Page in her mind and numbed by the swigs of Southern Comfort that Morris kept pushing on her from a silver flask, Nora capitulated to his back seat advances. *What the hell, why not. Give the poor sucker a break.*

The next day Mory applied for and was granted first shift work in the shop. He needed to see his conquest regularly. He gave up his lunch breaks to visit her in the office break-room. He brought her flowers, sweets and small gifts.

Nora accepted these offerings with pleasure and satisfaction although reluctantly, not wanting the others to recognize any special relationship between them. She never accepted Morris's pleas for a second date. Then one day she whispered in his ear, "I'm pregnant."

Morris and Nora were married on a cold and dark December afternoon. Morris Masters was as proud and as tall as he had ever been. Nora, surprised, detached and dreamy, was pulled from her reverie by the JP asking, "Will you, Nora, take this man . . . ?"

She had been thinking: *Jimmy. We'll call the baby Jimmy. And he will have long hair and play guitar Yes, Jimmy.*

~

When Nora left her husband and young son to fend for themselves ten years later, Morris seemed to shrink even smaller than his paunchy five foot five and one half inches. He had started drinking seriously years earlier in the sham marriage. He managed to keep his factory job another year after Nora left, then handouts and unemployment checks provided meager subsistence—enough for a daily fifth of rot-gut and little else.

"Dad. Dad! Wake up for chrissake. You puked on your shirt. Clean up. Go to bed."

Young Jim became the parent of his father. He dropped out of school. He took odd jobs with any tradesman who needed an extra pair of unskilled, low-paid hands. One day, not long after he turned 16, he discovered his father was gone, along with the few dollars he had earned and socked away in his bureau drawer.

~

In the pre-dawn grayness, First Sergeant Edmond Bonners, fondly known as Little Caesar or Black Eddy, called Private James Masters out of morning ranks waiting to march to the mess hall for breakfast.

Masters was hungry as he reluctantly answered Bonners' summons. "Here, First Sergeant!"

"Report to the C.O. on the double.

Captain Bruce O'Brien, commanding officer of Wolf Training Company, had joined the Corps after a brief career as a heavyweight boxer from which he retired undefeated. He was a career marine in his thirteenth year of service and had hoped to retire a full colonel. Now after two years as a recruit training officer, that happy circumstance seemed less likely.

"Private Masters reporting as ordered, Sir!"

O'Brien flipped a return salute. "At ease, Private."

He found it hard to believe that the husky young marine recruit standing on the other side of his desk was underage, just 16. "Private Masters, I am sorry to say that as of this moment you are no longer a Marine."

He watched Master's broad shoulders droop, and dismay rise in his eyes. Before the young recruit could object, he continued "You are guilty of falsifying statements on the Marine Corps Requirements questionnaires."

He flipped a page in the file on his desk. "Number one: you are not yet 17 years of age. Number two: You forged your high school diploma. There is no proof you attended high school, much less graduated."

"But . . . but, sir. Permission to speak?"

"Never mind objecting, Masters. I can't help you. The orders are here. You're out."

"But, I'm a good Marine. Look at—"

"Listen to me, Private. You will receive a General Discharge, effective immediately. Pack up. You will be escorted from the base in exactly one hour." *Damned shame,* he thought. "Dismissed."

"But it ain't fair. Sir. I ain't done nothin' wrong!"

Uncontrollable rage propelled Private Masters as he lunged at the captain. Pain dropped him in his tracks, as a massive right jab shattered two front teeth.

Three months before his 17th birthday, with $300 of termination pay in his pocket and a set of Marine Corp utility fatigues on his back, Jim Masters was without a home and without a job on the streets of San Diego. His jaw hurt. His ego was battered. A massive headache threatened to crush his skull.

~

MASTERS PRIVATE CONTRACTING: PAINTING, BUILDING, LANDSCAPING. The sign on his decrepit truck was faded and hard to read, like its owner. Nevertheless, his friendly manner and honest reputation were assets in convincing strangers to trust him with almost any small job that required a general handyman. His work was competent, and word-of-mouth recommendations secured a steady stream of odd jobs throughout the suburban neighborhoods, as well as occasional impromptu female companionship.

Because he worked throughout the city and its suburbs, it was not unusual for him to not remember when or why he had been at one particular site or another. Moreover, his memory had been quirky lately.

Jim frowned and squinted curiously in his rear-view mirror, searching the back seat of the truck. *What's there? Is something back there?* A dull headache crossed his forehead. He relaxed his tight grip on the wheel, seeking to will his inner peace to remain, hoping the headache would not become what he had come to call the bloody, black monster. It could disable him with pain.

~

He would be powerless to resist if the monster did come to possess him. He could not predict the monster's coming, always in the truck. He could not defray or delay the crippling, controlling pain. Still more distressing, he could not remember his eventual escape from it.

He would offer anything to appease the monster—try anything for relief. He would have bartered his soul to be rid of it. Perhaps he had.

Memory was like a heavy black shroud, yielding to his mental probes, deforming but not opening to reveal its contents. He feared stripping back the shroud lest the bloody black monster might lie within.

Fear of the monster enslaved him, fear of the pain that threatened to crush his temples when the monster seized his head, fear of the blood-red veil that blinded his eyes after— after . . . ?

That is when he had begged for release, before the blackness descended where memory could not reach. *Where are you from? What do you want from me?* He could only pray for the blessed lapse into oblivion.

His memory extended only to a reawakening, always parked in the truck, an awareness of the world around him slowly dawning. Then, he could not retrace how he had arrived at this strange place. He knew only that the pain was gone and that something was very wrong.

~

Driving west on the interstate, the bright sun attacked his eyes, triggering long sequestered memories. Jim's thoughts leapt back into his childhood: Little League, late afternoon, retreating back, back, back into left field chasing the high fly ball, then the blinding sun in his eyes, the ball falling, not fielded, at his feet.

"I did try, Mama!"

"You should have had it, Jimmy."

"But . . . the sun . . . ."

Masters knew the monster was with him now, in the truck. He swerved sharply, setting off a dissonant chorus of automobile horns while he crossed two lanes of interstate traffic, seeking the nearest off-ramp.

Just let me find a place to park and rest a little.

He eased the truck into a corner slot near the exit of an unfamiliar strip mall. His flannel shirt, drenched with sweat, stuck to his taut torso. Jim cranked down the truck window and waited, weary, his head resting on the steering wheel.

Long shadows of late afternoon softened and faded into the dim light of dusk. He shivered with a cold fear while he raised his eyes and watched the steady flow of vehicles to and from the lot, customers entering and exiting the lighted storefronts.

The monster touched him now. He'd known it would, of course.

Masters stepped down from the truck while ferocious pain took command of his mind and body. He reached behind the seat. No one observed him open the long, slim package. Returning to the driver's seat, he held the small caliber Winchester bolt-action close to his side. He mumbled a promise of appeasement. "I'll do it."

He selected a convenient human target in the rifle's scope and fired. One deadly shot. The target, a young woman in a brightly flowered dress, crumpled to the ground.

The monster whispered, "Good boy," and laughed with relief while hot tears fell from his eyes.

From Time to Time

I stood quiet and alone, away from the flood of soft white light that illuminated the casket resting like an obscene altar on the small raised stage. In my plain, dark suit I was comfortably absorbed into the gray shadows that seemed to flow like late evening fog away from the room's central feature to the edges and corners of the walled space.

In the past hours and days, my emotions had flowed like a rocky stream rushing onward, seeking still waters, moving erratically from a blinding explosion of shock and rage to the dull, numbing ache of grief that shunned all color and brightness.

Few had come tonight to pay their respects to the deceased and none remained to join my vigil for the dead. Perhaps the chilling early spring rain had kept some away. A shrunken little couple with matching heads of bright white hair had introduced themselves as our neighbors, Mr. and Mrs. Jameson. Thank God for the intro—I wouldn't have known them from the Addams Family.

Then there was the obligatory emissary from the multi-national company where Sonny had worked for twenty-five of the past twenty-six years who offered his cool, professional condolences. That lovely young woman on his arm seemed genuinely moved and solicitous though—what was her name, Monique, Marlene? She seemed to have known Sonny, though he had never mentioned her to me.

Only the thought of Sonny being alone with strangers kept me here now in spite of my weary depression at an hour when the morticians were anxious to close their doors to visitors and get on about their dismal business. Then surprise pushed aside my depression when a tardy visitor moved cautiously and hesitantly along the opposite wall finally stepping forward and standing illuminated in front of the open coffin.

My God, my dull mind reacted in slow recognition, *it's Frank.* His dark, wavy hair had gone gray, short and sparse. Gravity and time had modified his profile, tugging his chest downward toward his belt-line since I had seen him last, more than ten years ago, at the end of our short, sorry affair.

Frank stared intently at the pale, cold face of his one-time friend, Sonny, my dead husband, as if trying to read some clue or expression in the death mask. He crossed himself absently, turned away from the coffin and looked up as I moved toward him. Would he still recognize me? Time had not been unkind to my face and figure, but I had changed more than he in our decade as strangers.

His new little tummy made him less intimidating than the slim, angular Frank I had known when we had each found our own measure of satisfaction with the other. But when he looked up at me, those stark baby-blues were still the same as when he used to impersonate the famous Frank, singing the only song lyric he knew: *Make it one for my baby, and one more for the road.* I loved his voice.

"Joan?" He paused as recognition and realization seeped into his mind. "Joan, yes it's really you, Joan."

"Didn't you expect to see me here?" I swept a hand through my short 'apricot aura' hair and reached out toward him with the other.

He took my hand warmly between both of his. His eyes held mine, searching. Finally he whispered, "Well, yes, of course. But still. . . ." He shifted his gaze away from mine and dropped one hand awkwardly at his side as if self-conscious in front of the dead man behind him. "I came to offer my sympathy . . . and to see Sonny."

"Thanks Frank, we appreciate it. How have you been?"

His reply echoed my matter-of-fact tones. "Fine, still putting in my time for the company. I envy Sonny retiring when he did." He couldn't hide a shy grimace. "I, uh, guess that sounds rather stupid now. But, I mean I'm glad he got at least this past year for himself, and for you. What a crying shame it ended so quickly. Tell me what happened."

~~~

Sonny Wilson stepped into the warm morning, pulled the front door of the 1940s bungalow shut and tested the lock. It was a day to delight the senses and make the soul rejoice. Soft shafts of golden sunlight streaked through the early morning mist, painting golden globs on pink azaleas and lavender tulips. Honeysuckle floated their sweet scent in the light breeze. Hungry birds gave voice to wake-up calls—roisterous wrens, businesslike chickadees, and antisocial cardinals competing with the inharmonious jays.

Sonny did not see or smell or hear the glorious day. He watched his feet shuffling in scuffed brown loafers across the driveway, carefully avoiding the random, weed- filled cracks in the concrete. He listened hopefully as the starter ground in the gray, ten-year-old Volvo, and he smelled only the blue exhaust that spewed when the car sprang reluctantly to life and he backed down the driveway.

He paused in the vacant street, glanced at the shaded bedroom window and silently mouthed his daily invocation, "Have a good day, Sweetheart."

He pulled the gearshift into drive, wondering if they would be lucky enough to sidestep disaster again today, then started one more morning commute.

It would be his last.

~~~

The break room was almost deserted when Sonny arrived at the office. Glancing around, he noticed Frank Jackson and Tim O'Brien sharing a table. He emptied the thick, hot coffee dregs from the carafe into his cup and broke an onion bagel in half. He took a seat alone near the door to wait for his nine o'clock appointment.

Tim, the pain-in-the-ass, glad-hand promoter, Sonny thought. O'Brien was twenty years his junior, but he always treated Sonny, like most others, with borderline contempt. He kept a mental file on everyone in the office and took frequent pleasure in sharing his mental notes, without undue concern for truth or accuracy, with anyone who would listen.

But it was Frank Jackson who raised his hackles now. Frank and Sonny had started working for the company the same day, over twenty-five years ago. They had socialized at parties then, bowled together, were friends—until ten years ago.

Sonny stared at his coffee, steadying the steaming cup in his two large hands, surprised by the rush of pain and anger seeing Frank had brought. He repressed the pain that often gripped his chest and tore at the corners of his mouth. He pushed back the thoughts of those decade-old events; he had long ago become expert at that.

He forced his thoughts to the welcome monotony of his day's work as company photographer and part-time reporter. Nine AM: interview new department secretary. Ten: photo-op of the Big Man showing off for a handful of stock analysts. Have the photo proofs on Big Man's desk before 2 PM. Three: Process 9 o'clock interview into copy. Four: Call Joan.

O'Brien's booming baritone barged through Sonny's thoughts. "Hey Frank, what do you think of the new sec?"

"Which one?"

"Like you don't know who I mean? Martine! Drop dead gorgeous! With the long black hair and—good god, you can't have missed her legs."

"Ah, yeah, in accounting. She does make those miniskirts look good. I agree, I do indeed agree. Have you talked with her?"

Tim leaned in as if to speak in confidence, but his voice remained at broadcast volume. "Keeps pretty much to herself. Quiet. But she can be very funny."

Martine Rodriguez was Sonny's 9 o'clock appointment. New employee interviews were the least favorite part of his job. He would welcome anything to spark his profile of her in the division monthly newsletter.

"Funny in what way?" Sonny asked across the room.

O'Brian frowned in his direction, apparently annoyed by the interruption that might seem to question his veracity, but determined to share his notes, even with Sonny.

"She really cracks me up! She's a natural mimic. Like, she did that little swagger of the boss-man to a T. Riot. Bet she could even make you laugh, Sonny Boy."

Sonny resisted a reply to Tim's last remark. He checked his Timex. "Well, thanks for the preview. I'm off to see the little lady now."

He turned at the door to face the two men and mumbled, "See you around, Frank," and walked out, not expecting a reply nor receiving one.

When he found the Central Accounting office suite and glanced into the open door Sonny knew that O'Brien, at least this once, had not exaggerated. *Wow*, he thought. His voice was suddenly hoarse. "Mornin' miss, you are Martine?"

"Yeah, who wants to know?" Her question was careless and crass, but her voice was low and seductive, like a Coltrane blues note.

"Sonny," he said, "Sonny Wilson. I'm here for the interview."

He studied a framed print on the wall, purposefully and with great difficulty, avoiding staring at her.

"Oh, sure. They told me to expect it. Hang on a sec."

His eyes pulled against his will from the pastel print to her face, and he memorized her profile as she typed a few more lines.

She turned to him at last. "Aren't you a little old for a Sonny?" She flashed a smile, bright and impudent. He flushed involuntarily—dazzled, offended, and confused.

He searched for a bright answer to defend himself. *Got my work cut out here*, he thought, and decided to ignore her question. He cleared his throat. "It's painless, the interview. I just need a few lines for the company news. And a photograph. New employee feature. To introduce you to the company."

Those eyes will burn a hole in the page! She will have every stud in the company at her door after this little article.

"Okay, Son...ny." She stretched his name playfully, like a kitten playing with string. "Shoot." She watched attentively when he flipped open the stenographer's notebook.

"Name: Martine Rodriguez, right?"

"100 percent so far."

"Where are you from?" The standard questions came automatically.

"Native of D.C., heart of the city."

"Did you go to school there?"

"No. Oh yeah, preschool. Does that count?"

Sonny blinked at the floor. "High school or college?"

Her scent reached his nostrils as she leaned toward him, drawing his eyes briefly to hers. "We moved a couple of times after Dad lost his job at the post office," she said. "He drank."

Sonny scratched his ear with the Scripto. "Oh." He shifted in his chair and studied his notebook. A small stain of sweat dampened his shirtfront. "I just need a few facts for our personnel column. Nothing too detailed, you know?"

Martine shrugged and shot a glance at him that said "whatever." She said, "I hated school."

"Okay, but ..."

She cut him short. "I hated being a minority with the blacks. But they didn't bother me much. We're Mexican, couple of generations back, and French. Dark enough to pass for black, I guess."

She smiled that smile again, and her eyes dared his reply. Sonny squirmed. He groaned inwardly. *This will look great in print.*

Still ignoring his plea for brevity Martine spoke quietly to him, but now the challenge in her voice was gone. "You remind me of my father in a blond, green-eyed sort of way. My father died. Pop died. Killed, actually. A brawl, sort of."

Sonny pronounced each word slowly. "God, are you serious? Sort of a brawl?"

"Pop was much too passive to fight anyone. He was mooching drinks at a bar. Someone took offense. Beat the shit out of him, just for fun. He died."

Sonny flipped the notebook closed and matched her gaze steadily, seeing more than her beauty for the first time.

"I am sorry." He reached out involuntarily and stopped, under control. "Really sorry."

He wanted to comfort her, hold her, tell her he suffered with her. He said, "Listen, I have another meeting at ten. Maybe I could reschedule with you."

"Don't bother," she replied, flip and abrupt again. "I'm loaded with work today, and I'm out of here by four."

~~~

The analyst photo-shoot went well in spite of Sonny's distraction—the unfinished business with Martine that nagged his thoughts. Big Man was satisfied with the proofs, even complimentary, by god! But Sonny needed a wrap on the Rodriguez interview, with photos, by tomorrow afternoon. He made two phone calls.

"Central Accounting," she answered, "this is Martine."

Sonny explained his need to complete the interview. She refused to stay late at the office but offered an alternative. "I don't live far from the office. Why not come finish your interview at my place when you have time?"

His head spun. "I don't think I can do that." Finally, always seeking to comply and to satisfy both of their needs, he agreed to her suggestion and to finish his job at her apartment later in the afternoon.

"What the hell is so urgent that she can't stay an extra hour at the office?" he muttered. But her voice had stirred an excitement that did not fade as he gathered up film, cameras and lights. He wanted to see her again.

He made his second call. "Hi Hon." He hoped he sounded more calm than he felt. "Last minute crisis here. I need to finish this photo spread for Big Man. It may go into the annual report." It was only partly fabrication.

Joan answered, "Oh, sorry." She sounded clear and awake, no hint of narcotic fog. "Will you bring dinner?"

"No, I can't tell how late I'll be." He tried to picture her reaction—anywhere from a little pout of disappointment to a seething rage. Why had he not told her where he was really going? They didn't have secrets. Not anymore.

In the Volvo, he thought, *To hell with this, I'm going home.* Instead, he drove slowly, searching and finding his way on the city streets to Martine's apartment. He circled the building complex and finally parked in the street a half block away. He slung the equipment bag on his shoulder, grabbed his attaché case and walked quickly to find her apartment.

"Sorry I'm late," he said when she opened the door.

His pulse pounded in his ears. She had changed into denim cutoffs and a white blouse, nothing more. Washed of makeup and barefoot she appeared childlike and vulnerable.

"Hi Sonny. My, what a big bag you have." She reached to relieve him of the camera bag. "You look like the big, bad wolf."

"Let's get at it," he growled, as if taking the part, "I don't have long." She led him inside and through a small kitchen made smaller by the clutter of clean and unwashed items, apparently mixed at random.

"I'm not much of a homemaker," she whispered.

No crap, he thought, *Joan would puke if she saw this.*

The combined living and dining area was surprisingly neat, even though overburdened with books, CDs, videos, and magazines. "I read a lot," she said, "and opera turns me on."

He watched while she bent to adjust the volume down on the amplifier.

"Turandot?"

"Yeah, I love the Italians. Mostly Verdi and Puccini." She motioned him into a corner of the couch, and she sat facing him from the only chair. With her feet on the chair cushion she rested her folded arms on drawn-up knees, cocked her head and asked, "What's on your mind, Mr. Sonny Reporter?" She poised an imaginary pencil over an imaginary notebook. "Or is it Mr. Photographer now?" She pressed an imaginary camera to her eye. "Click."

Sonny laughed a weak, wooden laugh, but his tension eased away. The smile he tried on felt stiff on his face. Martine laughed aloud. "Poor baby, maybe you should get your photos now." She struck a mock glamour pose, lifting her long black hair off her shoulders and stretching her dark, straight legs in the air.

Before he could react she moved from the chair to the couch. Close and warm, her fresh-washed scent seduced him as no perfume would. She lifted the notebook and pencil from his hands and retreated to the chair again.

She flipped open the notebook with one hand, mimicking the motion she had watched him make at the office. "You're Thoney Wilthon," she said, exaggerating his nearly imperceptible lisp, "tell me about yourthelf."

He would have seethed at the mockery from someone else, but now he took no offense. He played along, drawn strangely into the game. "Yeth, okay."

She sat straight now, with counterfeit seriousness, the Scripto poised, ready to record. "Are you happy?"

"Ha. . .happy?" The question rocked him. "Yeah, sure, why not?"

"Let's start with something easier. Tell me about your wife. Do you have a wife?"

"Joan, she . . . ." He felt suddenly lost, unable to speak or continue his thought.

Martine's voice seemed distant. "Can't shut you up once you get going, can we?"

Sonny was hunched forward, his face in shadow. Muted, mumbled words issued slowly, painfully from his mouth. "We lost our son, you know. He was fifteen. Ten years ago." He straightened. "Ten years, for Chrisake!"

Martine looked long into his crumbling mask. She listened and learned about the sudden illness that destroyed the nervous system of their only child.

"His name was John. Bright, beautiful, sensitive and talented—like Joan. Three records in freshman swimming. Honors classes. We thought the fever and headache were from over-exertion. 'Rest,' we said. He was gone in forty-eight hours. He's resting now. Ten years."

Music strained from the Turandot CD. More tortured images came to play in his mind. "I didn't talk to anyone, started fights with everyone, almost got fired."

Finally freed from the suppressed grief of years, he continued. "The job didn't matter. Life didn't matter. No one mattered—no one but Joan. Poor Joan. I thought she was the strong one. I didn't know."

Sonny rose to his feet, swayed painfully front to back. "My pal Frank called me one night. 'Come get your wife, she's drunk again and wants to play.' I learned she had been looking for love in all the wrong places, sleeping around, boozing. Guess I was the last to know. She doesn't sleep around anymore. Took the cure too, but what does it matter? We both died then, as dead as John. We've been strangers ever since, sometimes worse than strangers."

Sweat and tears streaked his face. His eyes faded. Sonny Wilson was quiet at last.

Martine came to him, took his hands, kissed his lips. She led him to the bed and undressed him, then herself. Much later, at the door, she kissed him again, gently now, and said, "You're not near as dead as you thought, are you dear man. Go home Sonny. Go home to Joan."

~~~

Sonny's mind raced, once again in turmoil by the time he approached home. The peace and release he had found with Martine was gone. Turning into his drive, Sonny switched off the Volvo's headlights, but he did not turn off the engine. He sat waiting in the dim, gray light of pre-dawn. *Will anyone be surprised when I don't show up for work today? Will anyone give the tiniest little crap when they discover I'm not there?* He thought about the message he would leave. *Will Joan understand?*

He turned off the engine, opened the car door and stepped out. A soft, early morning rain had washed the landscape fresh and clean. A rusty wren spoke excitedly to him when he approached too close to her nest. "Okay flicker-tail," he said, "your babies are safe." He slipped off his loafers as he often did before entering the house and found himself dancing barefoot in the grass. Dancing! Barefoot. *If the Jamesons see me, they will call the cops.* He laughed until tears came to his eyes, inhaled deeply the sweet scent of honeysuckle, and quietly went inside.

Joan was asleep, curled up tight on the couch in the living room. She must have been waiting up for him. An open carton with half of an anchovy pizza was on the floor beside her with an empty can of Diet Coke. Her face appeared youthful and innocent in the muted television lighting that ebbed and flowed in silent waves; the usual lines of age and abuse were indiscernible.

Ah, Joanie. Do you remember our golden days? Will you, can you ever come back to me now, or are those days lost forever?

Sonny walked quietly to the kitchen phone where he called the office and left a message on the secretary's voice mail. "This is Sonny. I quit."

He found the calendar Joan kept on the counter. He drew a large, dark circle around the date. Inside the circle he wrote: *Strangers No More*. He returned to awaken his wife to begin their new life together. His broad and tranquil smile would be the first thing she saw that day.

~~~

Except for the undertaker, that gray, silent shadow that glided, always discretely at a distance, ready to offer solicitous assistance at the blink of any moist eye, Frank and I were alone with Sonny in the viewing chamber. I took Frank's arm—strong but wiry, not like Sonny's massive hams. Would he want to hear my confession?

"Let's sit down. Do you mind?" We sat tête-à-tête on a small divan at the side of the room. Softly, from discretely positioned speakers, an undying tape played *Rock of Ages*.

"I killed him, Frank."

Frank would not have known how, until fewer than twelve months ago, Sonny and I had walled each other out for most of the past ten years, laying brick upon brick of resentment and self-pity, finally adding futility and despair to the hardening mortar.

We had been happy until that nightmare started, ten years past. We had shared our love, our lives and fortunes.

We had warm friends and our private diversions, though we sought little for satisfaction beyond our small close family.

Rearing our beautiful, blond-haired boy magnified the love we shared and our happiness.

Then we lost him, our only son John, at age fifteen, and we couldn't remember a world without him, as if there had always been the three of us, loving, sharing. We couldn't remember or tolerate a retrospective world of two.

A violent rage of infection, meningitis probably, killed him in forty-eight hours, killed our only child. The triangle collapsed. I didn't know how to mend the broken link, how to be again what we once had been, just Sonny and me, friends and lovers.

I said, "Frank, you remember how Sonny was after John died. Belligerent, withdrawn, sullen . . . even with me . . . or especially with me. Not that I helped him any. I nearly destroyed him with my sleeping around."

Frank knew this. Frank, more than anyone, knew how I had turned to booze when Sonny wasn't there for me, and from booze I had turned to sex.

His eyes darkened now. Maybe he hadn't known he was only one of those who had provided brief, intense, impersonal relief from my burning sorrow. Sex was my morphine, but Sonny wasn't providing it. Sonny had turned quietly inward to deny his grief; and he had left me outside and alone.

"You turned me in," I said, "remember? You called Sonny to come and take me home. I guess you needed to polish up your tarnished honor. I know I didn't mean anything to you—just an easy lay."

Frank folded his arms and sat back, moving away from me. "Come on," he said, "you got what you wanted from me. Maybe I seemed easy, but you were hard to resist. We both knew it was a mistake. But I did care for you then, and for Sonny. I still do."

"No need to be defensive, Cool Frank." I touched his arm. "You did the right thing when you ended it. It sure got Sonny's attention. He didn't blame me, and he was actually grateful to you. He tried to help me then."

Phantom details, scratching and gnawing for recognition, had invaded my mind since Sonny died three days ago. Now I flushed with anger re-ignited. "But after that he watched, watched and hovered. God, he hovered.

He spent every possible minute with me, eating, sleeping, talking—screaming. He had to work, of course, for a living and for his sanity. That's when I drank."

~~~

"Leave me the fuck alone you son-of-a-bitch!" I heard my words echoed over the years.

"Okay . . . okay. How about something to eat?" Sonny's voice was calm, but the veins in his temples bulged and throbbed.

"Fuck you! Eat yourself!" I wanted to rip his guts, to make him bleed. I wanted him to hurt.

"Please babe, we need help," Sonny's words came snotty-wet. He slumped forward on his knees, trying to hold me in his grasp. My fists slammed his broad back and his bowed head with all the strength my booze-soaked, stuporous state allowed, until my arms flailed thin air, my eyes clamped shut, my head hung back and I laughed. "Victory!"

~~~

Now, I edited that scene for Frank. "Sonny tried to keep the booze away from me. He tried to get me professional help. I resisted. I refused. I was determined to beat him, to show us both that I could survive without him, without anyone. After a couple of years our struggle became a bloodless ritual, without emotion—without hope."

Why didn't he leave me? Why did the silly bastard hold on so, after hope was gone? I just didn't get it. I had asked the question again and still again. One day when the alcohol fog was less dense than usual the answer came in the form of another question. Is this what love is? That's when I went to the clinic to kill the demon rum.

"I haven't had a drink in four years, Frank. The clinic fixed my drinking, but it didn't fix Sonny and me. We were strangers living in the same house—until one day a year ago, when it seemed we had sucked our souls dry. That day changed everything."

That day a miracle happened. A soft rain fell, spring flowers bloomed, the birds sang. When the morning sun broke through with a promise of warmth and brightness, Sonny sat beside me, and his first touch woke me. I knew then that we were husband and wife again. So did he.

"I just quit," Sonny said and smiled his quiet, certain smile. "I quit my job today—by voice mail!"

He laughed, and so did I. I touched his shining face, fingertips moving, gliding over the mounds of his lips, his crooked nose, and along his brows, closing the lids on his gentle, tired eyes.

"Good for you, Sonny. What should we do today?"

And we laughed again and held each other in the new light of a new day.

One golden day followed another. We discovered each other again, more fully than the first time. We discovered the world and all its grand and tiny miracles. We read each other's thoughts. We cherished every new moment, every new and every passing season, from spring into winter.

Frank's face became an expression of concern when I continued. "A few weeks ago Sonny became pensive, nervous, withdrawn. He spent hours—days—paging through our checkbook or reading legal papers. He could get so compulsive. 'Do the job right. Do the best that you can do. Finish what you start.' His favorite mottos."

Frank nodded and offered an unnecessary prompt. "What was he doing?"

"He was checking files and making lists. Finally, I got him away from the house. I begged him, 'Come on, hon, give yourself a break. Whatever are you busting your hump on? Give me a little time. Let's go to Rock Cliff for a picnic.'"

I closed my eyes and all the magic and mayhem of that day came vividly into my mind.

Sonny had sparked like a boy skipping school. "Great idea! It's been years. Wonder if that beat-up picnic basket is still around?"

An hour later, we had the blanket spread near the summit of the cliff, just down the grassy slope enough to break the chilling spring breeze that buffeted the rocky cliff to windward. No one else was there. We cuddled. We talked, we laughed. Sonny got another blanket from the car and underneath, urgently, like teenagers, we made love while the tuna sandwiches, boiled eggs, dill pickles and iced tea waited and wilted.

"I love you, Joanie girl," he whispered in my ear while I pulled my clothes back in order.

"I love you too, Sonny boy." It was the expected response in a short dialogue that had once been routine for us. "But I'm starving! Break out the picnic basket before you get any more ideas." I might have giggled thirty years earlier.

Sonny pulled out Melmac plates and cups, clear plastic knives and forks, and bright cotton napkins. He rummaged in the bottom of the basket. "What the hell? Look at this."

He held a pint bottle of Smirnoff 100 proof, a forgotten cache from the years when I could pull an emergency drink from at least half a dozen hiding places.

"Sorry, babe," I said, "guess that one got away. Just pitch it over the cliff."

Instead, he twisted off the cap and held the bottle up in two hands, like a priest raising the chalice in communion. He held the bottle to his lips and drank deeply. He downed nearly half the pint in thirsty gulps. What the hell was he doing—he hadn't had a hard drink in all the years I had known him? Another slug went down before he dropped the bottle at his side, looking as surprised and stupefied as I felt watching him. The clear vodka spilled, soaking the red blanket to a dark, blood-like stain.

Sonny struggled to his feet. He hiccupped. "Sorry." His face had that silly, apologetic grin that meant plastered. The booze had hit his virgin brain like a soggy, dense, blinding fog. The smile he tried to smile turned into a caricature, a World War II cartoon of Japanese Emperor Hirohito smiling, with front teeth protruding over his lower lip. "So solly, babe. So solly, please."

He performed a deep, obsequious bow, nearly pitching forward into the pickles and tuna and me. That, he seemed to think, was hilarious. He giggled and hooted and interspersed a string of silly laughs with "So solly, so solly please."

His elaborate bows were studiously balanced now, deep concentration showed on his face, alternating with a mindless grin.

I was between amused and alarmed, but I laughed with him. "Sonny, for God's sake sit down, you're going to kill yourself."

The grotesque grin faded from his flushed face, replaced first by a blank, demented stare, then by a quizzical frown of determination so fierce I had to laugh again. He raised his arms and stood at attention, looking from my perspective like Christ the Redeemer on Mount Corcovado.

He lurched forward into a trot, circling the picnic blanket, arms held out stiffly. "Kamikaze," he blurted, "Kamikaze. So solly." He staggered past me, up the slope toward the cliff, looking like a great lumbering albatross accelerating for takeoff.

"Kamikaze!" His drunken scream reached me, carried in the wind, while I watched him step out over the edge of the cliff and disappear toward the rocks below.

~~~

That nightmare vision brought me back to the present, and I shared the essentials of those recollections with Frank. He remained silent, slowly shaking his head.

I said, "It was mine of course, the vodka. Long forgotten and unwanted. Sonny didn't drink, never had. Why did he open it? Why did he drink it? I will never forgive myself. I will never forgive him. How could he make such an idiotic mistake?"

Finally, choking sobs came with tears that spilled my grief and wetted Frank's lapels. I turned and opened my eyes to look at the coffin, isolated and unadorned under the floodlight. *Talk to me, you bastard. Why?*

Frank's voice was soft, and he spoke as if answering my thoughts. "Listen to me, Joan. I met Sonny last week. We hadn't talked for ten years, maybe more. But, he phoned me and sounded urgent—not desperate, but compelling."

"He didn't mention it to me," I said.

"No, he wouldn't have. I don't think he knew many people he could talk to, but he knew from the office that I'm a paralegal. He wanted to be sure you had help and support."

"Help for what?"

"He knew he was going to die."

"My God! What are you saying?"

"Sonny was terminal. He thought he had a couple of months before the cancer would put him down. He hated the thought of being an invalid, and dependent."

I staggered to my feet and pounded my closed fist on the wall again and again and again, as I had pounded Sonny years ago. I turned to plead with Frank. "Why didn't he tell me?" I sobbed, "He didn't tell me."

"He was thinking how to break it all to you. We had planned a final meeting today before he talked to you about his estate."

Frank stopped, bit his lip uncertainly, took my hands in his again. "His accident was a fluke." He stumbled on the word *accident*. "Your picnic was unforeseen. The vodka was a shock. Who knows what he thought? Maybe he saw a way out, an easier way for everyone."

The onerous thought that Sonny's final act may have been intentional was not one I could accept easily. Finally I raised my eyes to look at Frank. "He was always the considerate one, right. Wait for me here . . . please."

I stepped up to Sonny's side and looked for a long while at the face I had loved so in the springtime of our life together and had grown to love even more in our final year. How quickly the time of those last seasons had passed. I mussed his thin blond hair. So many years wasted.

Fragments of another Sinatra lyric played in my head: *Regrets, we had a few . . . We did what we had to do . . . We loved, we laughed and cried . . . But now as tears subside.*

My hand was calm, resting on Sonny's. "We did our best, Sonny Boy. We did the best that we could do. It's all that we could do. We did it our way."

I felt release and reconciliation wash over me as if an angelic hand had touched me. Then I felt suddenly and desperately tired. My vision dimmed and my step faltered as I moved down and away from the box that would hold my Sonny in his eternal interment. Another hand caught me to prevent my collapse and guide me gently from the room. Frank.

Outside the rain had ceased and a fresh breeze blew.

"I'll drive you home," Frank said.

"It's out of your way. I'm okay, really. I can manage."

"I really want to Joan. Not as if anyone is at home waiting for me."

We drove in silence, perhaps individually and unknowingly sharing the same thoughts. The car radio reported the storm had passed. Tomorrow the overcast would yield, the sunlight of springtime would return to warm the land.

Picture Window

Her name is Leona. Her feet and legs are bare. A short, satin robe covers her, draping softly on the curves of her still-shapely body. Her eyes reflect dull green in the glass of the picture window, vaguely focused on the scene that lies before her from the second story of the remodeled old farmhouse.

She squints, absently twisting a strand of tangled red hair, looking out over a blinding white expanse of snow-covered fields edged by rolling hills and outlined here and there by the thin gray branches of distant, leafless trees. The overcast sky resists the feeble morning sun; on the pale horizon it blends seamlessly with the fresh white terrain.

Now and then a form or movement near the tree line catches her attention—the old man or the boy or something or someone not clearly distinguished. As she turns from the glass, a single gunshot echoes back to the house. She jerks her head toward the sound and gasps involuntarily.

Her moving gaze catches the blur of her reflected image. The lines that have invaded her youthful face are hardly visible in the soft reflection, nor are the brimming tears that well suddenly. She shivers, urgently cold. She folds her arms below her breasts and pads quickly across the cold, plank floor to her bedroom. She dresses haphazardly in articles selected at random from those littering the floor before returning to her lonely vigil.

~

The house awakened early that morning when the alarm sounded not long after dawn. As it always did, the alarm provoked a series of long, mournful howls from Bogart, the lanky black hound. Bacall, the longhaired golden retriever ran first in tight circles, then from Bogart's side to the old man's closed bedroom door and back again.

The door opened momentarily and the man appeared, eyes still fogged with sleep. His torn and faded plaid wool nightshirt hung loosely, accentuating his thinness. At the picture window he lifted the binoculars from their storage hook, wiped a sleeve across his eyes and raised the glasses to study the bleak horizon at the edge of the fields he once had farmed.

He spotted the intruder quickly and turned to call Billy, but the boy was already at his side, yawning like a cat, electrostatic repulsion from the dry, winter air splaying his blond hair like an erratic fountain. "Over there," Virgil said, and passed the glasses to the boy.

Billy raised the glasses, following the direction of the old man's nod. The boy was suddenly awake and enthusiastic. "Let's get him!"

Virgil knew it would be futile to protest or argue the boy's plea, that he would persist until successful. "You feed the dogs and load the guns while I dress and heat some coffee. Hurry now."

The alarm had wakened the woman too, but she lingered in bed, not interested in the scraps of conversation that filtered through her closed door. She shifted to her back and stretched. Her eyes found an amber stain on the ceiling, the telltale remnant of a one-time leak. William had repaired the roof leak, how many years ago? But the stain remained, unpainted, like a blot of dried blood.

Depression had stolen her memories, a day at a time, until the ugly ceiling spot was one of the few things that recalled William to her mind—except for the boy.

Her mind had learned to shun memories of her dead husband, but now in their bed she embraced the pain of recollection. At least it was a rare diversion from the hollow existence her life on the farm had become. She moaned, feeling William's gentle hands on her stomach and her thighs.

The downstairs door slammed shut when her son and father-in-law went out, shattering her unfulfilled living dream. She was alone again in the quiet house. She moved her legs over the edge of the bed, rose slowly and slipped into the little satin robe William had once loved.

~

The ground beneath the fresh snow cover was lightly frozen, ideal for tracking. The old man and the boy walked comfortably, speaking economically when they spoke, of sports and matters of low consequence, as if their purpose was no more than a leisurely Sunday morning stroll. They held their long guns by their dull, blue barrels, resting the stocks on their shoulders. Bogey and Bacall trotted loosely at their side. They passed the old International, rusting and abandoned in the field since William had gone away to war.

The old man said, as he had a hundred times before, "Your dad invented that alarm, Billy."

William, Virgil's only child, had conceived the alarm and installed it long ago, years before his tactical support reserve unit was called to active duty.

"Hooked up the old electric fence power supply to IR motion detectors. Used the detectors to trigger the alarm in the house. Damned clever, your dad was—wanted the alarm to let him know there was wildlife around to watch

119

or photograph. But he never was much for hunting and killing."

The old man stopped and spat. The pungent brown stream streaked towards Bogart. The lanky dog had learned to be wary of the old man's habit and quickly veered without losing stride.

"I can't remember him much," Billy said. The old photographs helped keep his memories alive, of course. Wedding photos of his father in a black suit and his mother in a white dress—a handsome couple all agreed. Photos of William, shirtless, waxing a shiny new Chevrolet, showing his broad shoulders and brawny arms. Photos of his mother, pregnant and radiant. Photos of himself in a too-big baseball cap, sitting on his father's shoulders. Photos his father had taken of deer and fox and nesting birds and even one black bear waving at the telephoto lens.

Billy had observed the once-bright, color photos age year-by-year, taking on faded casts of pink and lavender. Many were soiled and creased from his mother's desperate handling after the call that told her William, her beloved husband, would not return to her alive. Billy had saved them all, but Leona never looked at them now.

Billy tried to prompt his grandfather to speak again, to share details of a time at the edge of his own recollection. "I can remember how Daddy loved to watch the deer in the fields and the wild turkeys at the edge of the woods, and Mom would walk with him carrying grain for the animals in the winter. That was before you started putting out salt blocks and corn, before you taught me to hunt."

The old man did not respond, but pointed in the direction they should proceed and pressed a finger to his thin lips. They had come to the creek where the first alarm sensor was located. All the migrant and native animals used the creek as their super highway to move quickly from one point to another. It was an essential water supply too, though now the flow was very slow and crusted with a paper-thin layer of ice.

The boy paused, then with youth's casual agility he jumped to a large, central rock and again to the opposite bank. Virgil walked on and crossed slowly, using his shotgun as a makeshift cane to balance carefully on the smooth trunk of a fallen maple that bridged the shallow stream.

They came together again twenty yards downstream, and the boy spoke again in an urgent whisper, pursuing his need to know if his memories were real. "Remember how different Mom was then? When she laughed it made me feel all warm. Now she doesn't hardly smile, or talk even, 'cept to herself. I miss her, Granddaddy." He cleared his throat before his voice could break into a sob. "Will she ever smile or laugh again?"

"Can't talk no more," Virgil whispered in reply, "get ready." He carried an old Winchester twelve gauge shotgun, over-and-under. He broke open the breech to check the load in the chambers—slug on top, shot under. The slug could bring down a bear if fired accurately within forty yards. The load of shot would be good for small game—rabbits or birds. With his son no longer there to provide income or object to the hunt, he had been free to take game again. He had taught his grandson the basics of stalking, shooting and gun safety.

"You direct the dogs now," he instructed Billy quietly, "and check your rifle."

The boy knew the chamber of his Remington lever-action deer-rifle carried a steel-tipped thirty caliber round, and he had a fully loaded magazine. He checked the weapon now in deference to his grandfather. "Okay,"

The dogs stood still, sniffing the cold air, watching and waiting. Billy raised his arm and said, "Go!" Bogey and Bacall took off silently and swiftly, intent on circling and driving whatever game they might encounter back toward the two hunters.

The old man and the boy separated, now quiet, careful and alert, focused on the hunt, guns ready. They moved apart at the base of the hillock that separated them from a small open meadow where salt and corn enticed the whitetails to visit. To avoid showing themselves at the summit, Virgil bore left around the base of the hill while Billy circled right.

Billy skirted the hill first, raised the Remington and immediately fired once.

The young buck had no experience with the hunt, and the feast of grain he consumed now dulled his natural wariness. He raised his head and small rack high, sensing danger too late as Billy raised his rifle and brought his sights to bear. The high caliber shell entered behind his raised ear and tore through his head before his poised muscles could respond in flight. He dropped where he stood.

The dogs broke from the woods. They raced to the fallen deer. They watched the dying legs twitch as if trying to escape death, and with their muzzles between their front paws, lay down to wait for the old man and the boy.

~

The woman, dressed in faded green sweats and white, fluffy slippers, stood again watching at the window. She rarely dressed in proper clothes or left the house now, not even to roam the fields and forests of the old farm as she had so often done with William and little Billy.

Sunlight broke through the overcast from time to time, glinting off the crusted snow. Two figures moved side by side in the bright white landscape, dragging something behind them, making a jagged trail through the snow. Two dogs slouched silently trailing the laboring pair and their burden.

She watched the small spectacle approach, but the scene before her faded and then transformed. The snowy panorama changed to desert sand and the rusty truck morphed into a military tank. The moving figures waved to her, pointing at the gutted carcass they dragged behind, each holding onto one of the branched antlers. But the shouting, smiling men she saw wore foreign uniforms, and the bloody carcass they dragged was . . . "Oh, God," she shrieked, "William!"

She turned from the window and crumbled to her knees on the cold floor.

~

The old man and the boy slept late the next morning, exhausted and fulfilled by their outdoors adventure the day before. The buck hung, draining, head down behind the shed, ready to take in for butchering later in the week. It would provide meat for the table for many weeks to come.

The house was quiet, no alarms sounded. Bacall had stirred when the farmhouse door squeaked shut at dawn. Watching the pink-robed figure walk towards the distant line of trees she smudged the picture window with her wet nose. She whimpered once, then returned to lie beside Bogart on the floor.

Sometime later one brief, aborted note rasped in the alarm and quickly died unheeded, not sound enough to disturb the canine or human occupants of the quiet house.

At noon Billy lazily searched the house looking for his mother. He walked outside and saw new tracks leading away from the door. "I'm going out to look for Mom," he called to Virgil, and he started to follow the tracks made by bare feet in the snow. Bogart and Bacall followed at a slow trot, tails limp, unwilling to take the lead.

They found her at the creek.

Running forward, Billy called out, "Mom, Mom, what are you doing?" His voice cracked with fear and excitement. He slipped and stumbled on the frozen ground, almost falling at the creek bank.

She sat with her back to the frozen bank, legs extended in the frigid, shallow stream with a bare wire from the alarm power supply held tightly in one blackened hand.

Billy jumped into the creek bottom, splintering the fragile ice. He pulled her slumping head erect. Her cheeks had the same rosy hue as the crumpled, faded photograph in the frozen grasp of her other hand, the photo of a young man in military dress uniform. A serene smile lingered on her cold, lifeless face.

~

Now the alarm no longer sounds to alert Bogey and Bacall. Virgil had not objected when Billy carted the power transformer off to the dump. Still sometimes, late on moon lit nights or in the vague light before dawn, Billy awakes suddenly and goes to watch with the dogs at the picture window. Sometimes in the distant shadows he is sure he sees a tall, strong man walking hand-in-hand with a smiling, red-haired woman.

Richard Allen Anderson

Collateral Damage

The mouse hung head-down, pawing frantically at the air in front of its nose, suspended by the tip of its tail between the carefully manicured forefinger and thumb of Sergeant Henry Binder. Its tiny front feet were pathetically inadequate to defend against the hungry ten-foot python coiled just inches below, yet it fought for its life while primordial fear pumped blood frantically into its primitive brain and clouded its wild, gaping eyes. The small, white body twisted and swung while the python's head rose slowly to its prey.

"No, no, Mama. Not Junior. Not yet. Not today." Binder's voice oozed like honey as he lifted the smaller of his pets out of harm's way. He lowered Junior into an empty, quart pickle jar and screwed on the perforated cover. He placed the glass mouse-prison in a corner of the large, terrarium that housed Mama and closed the heavy lid. He watched the primitive, hunter-prey drama until Mama tired of pressing her cold nose against the invisible shield between her and Junior, and the mouse no longer jumped with fright, but lay shuddering and exhausted in a puddle of mouse urine.

It was a slow day in Wolfgang Kaserne. Most weekends were. No special training, no parade for visiting brass or politicians, not even the rare, surprise inspection that had never caught Sergeant Binder off-guard. As ranking noncom in the barracks, he kept his company of postal clerks on high alert for inspections. No messy lockers, no secreted porn, no un-made bunks—not on Henry Binder's watch.

Binder felt certain that his company attracted every oddball, every fuckup, and every Section-Eight-In-Waiting in the U.S. Army, European command. He accepted this challenge, and he addressed it frequently.

Holding his charges at attention in ranks, his strained, tenor voice sang out, struggling for attention. "You men will abide by the rules of this man's army or answer to me!"

He delivered orders in shrill, excited shrieks, like a demanding housewife. He put the un-compliant on report for unpolished brass, unshaven chins, and un-shined shoes. In short, he was a pain in the ass to both his superior officers and those he had the power to harass.

Pain-in-the-ass was a significant upgrade in status for Henry. At school, he had no friends, male or female. He had never been a team player, not even chess or debate club. Henry who? Few were aware of his existence. The few that knew him might have thought it odd that he enlisted in the United States Army, but his motivation was simple. He did not seek to fight for freedom or hide from the law or escape a relationship as many others did. He joined the Army to find a comfortable home.

~

Henry had known only one home until then, the one that his mother provided for him. He knew of no other living relative. Mrs. Binder, as everyone including Henry called her, taught physical education at the local, all-girls school where her propensity for regimentation was legendary. Other predilections, involving various young girls in her charge, were less well known.

Beatrice Binder managed her life prudently and rarely made an error. Henry was one of them, the result of her one college encounter with a member of the opposite sex. She tolerated the thing that had intruded itself into her body but made little accommodation for it in her solitary life. Beatrice went on with her college life much as she had before the unfortunate conception, attending classes and competing in track meets. Her trim and muscular figure was hardly altered as she approached the completion of her studies and graduation day. Neither her coach nor her professors became aware of the extra burden she carried. She neither sought nor received counsel or assistance for her situation. She had no desire to become a single mother, but her world view did not allow her to consider abortion to correct her error.

Henry was born in mid-summer, between Binder's graduation from Kensington College and the beginning of her teaching career. Beatrice secured a teaching contract with the high school, listing her status as divorced, one dependent. She rented a small, two-bedroom house, near enough to the school for a brisk, daily walk to work. She lived frugally, her only indulgence the packet of white powder she obtained from time to time in the girls' locker room at school.

Her neighbor, Old Mrs. T, minded Henry during the day until he was old enough to enter school. At home, Henry minded himself while Mrs. Binder watched television or performed occasional household duties, and sometimes snorted a bit of the white powder.

Beatrice tolerated Henry kindly, fed him and trained him. From time to time, as Henry developed from toddler into young boy, she held him erect in front of her, appraising his progress, and often wondered if a dog might have been less bother and of greater value.

Mrs. Binder trimmed her own short, dark hair the first Sunday of every month. Henry waited in warm anticipation for his turn to be groomed. Seated on the high kitchen stool,

Henry loved the touch of his mother's hands as she moved his head from side to side, buzzing his blond curls to a stubble, uniformly one eighth inch in length. He felt sheltered and secure under the big bath towel that draped his narrow shoulders.

Once, while the droning shears and the familiar action gave him a sense of quiet contentment he so seldom felt, Henry was emboldened to say, "All the other kids have Daddies. Who's my Daddy?"

Mrs. Binder looked away from the small boy's head toward the television that played silently on the kitchen counter. She watched absently as Monster Man body-slammed his opponent. She felt Henry squirm under the pressure of her hands.

"Don't we have a good life, just you and me?" she asked finally. "Don't I take care of you just fine? We don't need no Daddy to cause trouble and bother us, do we? Now go to your room and practice your numbers. And don't ask me any more silly questions."

Henry grew into a chubby version of Robert Redford, with shaggy blond hair falling over his green eyes. The crew-cut ritual had ended years ago, but he had learned that asking questions could be hazardous, and his reluctance to challenge authority grew as he did.

He passed from one grade to the next without distinction, neither bad nor good. The quiet small boy morphed into a dull young man, always in the shadows never the spotlight. He attracted neither friend nor foe. He was neither liked nor disliked by classmates, but rather, unnoticed.

His teachers and counselors offered little more attention until his graduation from County High approached. Then they seemed to notice him for the first time; the system required their final report. They interviewed and prodded him with questions but could not provoke his thoughts regarding vocational aspirations. Henry resisted their attention and suspected them of lacking any compassion, feeling or common sense when they suggested he might leave home to go to college.

Then Mrs. Binder died, not yet forty years old. Just weeks after Henry's graduation and before he had any notion which course his commencement journey might take, he was adrift and floundering.

~

The Persian Gulf War ended on the day Henry was sworn into the Army. He flourished in basic training, managing to complete it without injury or incident. He shed his flabby softness, benefiting from the daily calisthenics, forced marches and diet-wise mess hall meals. His body became taut and trim and his mind focused. His mission in life became clear. After only weeks of Army training, Henry Binder found something to love—military discipline.

He loved the spit and polish, company inspections and regimental parades. His uniforms were laundered and neatly pressed with sewn creases and tailored tucks. His reticence and stiffness often passed for military bearing. He eagerly conformed and complied—"Yes Sir. As you say, Sir."

Some might call it kissing brass. It was Private Binder's assurance of inconspicuousness.

After basic training, there were no major military conflicts. Binder's assignments were routine and undemanding. His army commanders sensed no leadership qualities beneath the soldierly veneer.

After ten years of duty, Henry took pride in a career that others might view as banal. He took his satisfaction, not in the military camaraderie of battles fought and survived in scattered corners of the globe, but in the rules and regulations that directed every aspect of his life and his relationships with others.

When renewed conflict drew others to serve in search and destroy missions in Afghanistan or to fight insurgents in the battle for Iraqi Freedom, Binder gratefully accepted assignment to the 55th Postal Company, 414th Base Support Battalion, in Germany. When he finally earned promotion to Sergeant, his stripes enabled his pissant sense of purpose; he stood vigilant and on constant guard for transgressions against his beloved military regulations.

~

Binder sat alone with Junior and Mama. The weekend would be ending soon. The others would return reluctantly from the shops and American bars in Hanau or the cafés and brothels of Frankfurt to the barracks they shared. Binder waited patiently. He knew he would have more interesting victims than Mama and Junior to torment before lights-out on this Sunday evening in May.

"Sergeant Binder report to HQ orderly room," the intercom squawked, "Binder to the orderly room!"

Binder's fatigue uniform was as spotless and pressed as his class A's. He had not shaved this morning, but after a quick chin-rub, he decided that answering the call immediately would have to take preference over his appearance. Promptness was near the top of his many virtues.

Binder read the name on the shirt of the corporal on duty in the orderly room. Smith. "What is it, Smith?"

"Replacement Private Hagerman is here." Smith gestured to the figure slumped and apparently asleep on the bench against the wall. "He's all yours. Get him outa here before the CO walks in."

Binder bristled at receiving orders from a subordinate rank, but he did not confront the issue He glanced at the sleeping replacement, uncertain how to proceed.

"Okay, Corporal Smith. Can you wake him for me?"

~

Hagerman was dog-tired, but he was not asleep. He was full of the stench and grime of three days travel without shower, shave or sleep. He had left the States with two hundred other graduates of his infantry basic training unit. Like them, he was willing and eager to join a fighting unit anywhere American troops were deployed. There were dozens of army infantry units in Iraq and Afghanistan, along with marines and airborne, even Rangers and Special Forces.

He had learned to shoot and kill for twelve weeks in the hills and swamps of Fort Benning. What in hell was he doing in Germany assigned to a frigging post office? One more outrage added to all the others he had endured over the past three months.

~

Aaron Hagerman had been known as "Ox" before he joined the army in response to the terrorist attacks on his homeland. The name exemplified his plodding, massive strength and his unresponsiveness to authority and direction except from the most skilled of his teachers or most beloved of his family. But it belied the intellect that was camouflaged by Aaron's reticence and by the dull look of his dark, deeply pitted face—an intellect that accepted no truth as self-evident and no authority as exempt from challenge.

Hagerman knew the extent of his strength and the benefits or dangers it could present to others. When the John Deere had slipped into gear and rumbled toward his unsuspecting father, Aaron threw a running block into it that diverted its deadly progress and tipped it up on one wheel. He had broken three of his football coach's ribs in demonstrating a body block for his high school teammates. He knew enough never to strike out in anger. He might kill someone.

At the first, pre-dawn muster at boot camp, before the company barbers had shorn each recruit head to G.I. stubble, Hagerman was renamed. A perceptive company clerk pushed back the long, shaggy mane covering Hagerman's averted eyes and drawled, "Well, looka-here, we got a damned Bison."

The dub was apt and stuck, capturing more precisely Hagerman's shaggy, rangy appearance—powerful shoulders, neck, and head—but especially the wild, trapped, mournful look in his wide, black eyes, like the eyes of a hunted and endangered animal.

Trusting in military discipline to tether the beast they perceived, Aaron's training cadre amused themselves testing the limits of his great strength and tolerance. He became the company beast-of-burden, toting extra heavy equipment on his back during long bivouac marches. He attracted extra quarter-mile runs when his plodding pace brought him to finish last in races that offered no positive reward except completion. From corporal to captain, his leaders always gave him special attention, as if daring some rebellious response:

"Bison! Put down that book and gimme twenty pushups—you ain't in college here!"

"Too slow, twenty more!"

"Bison, scrub that latrine floor again. Here's a new toothbrush."

"We can't decide whether you're dumber than you're ugly, or uglier than you're dumb. Are you dumber, Bison, or uglier? Answer me, Bison! Make up your mind, Bison! Louder, Bison!"

Reason, not fear, checked Hagerman from destroying his tormentors. He resolved to live through the nightmare of abusive and incompetent leadership. He would endure this world that was ruled not by logic and judgment but by blind obedience to commands.

He determined to learn the methods of warfare well, in his own interests and those of his country. He willed himself to lay aside all challenges to stupidity, intolerance, and incompetence. He learned the skills of armed and unarmed combat. He pulled his silent, sullen personality ever closer about himself, like his olive-drab rain slicker, as shelter from inclement insult and abuse. He endured. He waited. He forced himself to rationalize the torments he had tolerated in training as having some purpose. Yet his sequestered rage would not disappear.

~

Corporal Smith refused Sergeant Binder's request to wake Hagerman by saying he had other business to attend to. "He's your business now. Go shake him yourself, and take him with you."

Binder bristled again at Smith's brush off. He had asked politely, hadn't he? He walked over to confront Private Hagerman. Absorbing the appalling sight in small doses, he glanced at the huddled soldier, then away, then back again. Hagerman's unfortunate appearance was more than he could tolerate. There could be no excuse for this, travel or no travel. No hat. Torn trousers. Boots scuffed and caked with materials of indeterminate age and origin.

This hulking, unkempt brute is an unholy affront to me and to the United States Army. I'd better straighten this out right now.

The tendons in Binder's extended neck bulged as he leaned forward and screamed, red-faced and out-of-control, at the weary Bison. "Get up you sickening slob! Don't think I am going to help you drag that disgusting duffel into my barracks. Get up and stand at attention while I explain a few things to you about what goes in my outfit and what doesn't. Stand up before I report your sorry ass for insubordination!"

But it was Sergeant Binder's ass that suddenly pointed skyward while his mauve-colored, close-cropped head rested on the cold, concrete floor in front of his sewn-creased knees, and his wet, faded green eyes stared blankly at the grubby, greasy boots of his assailant, Private Aaron Hagerman.

His beating had been brutal, but swift. Then he went to black after one heavy boot crashed viciously into and through his lower rib cage, breaking bone and expelling the air he had been so desperate to inhale. He did not hear Hagerman's hoarsely whispered imprecation, "Happy Mothers' Day, Sergeant Asshole."

Hagerman's sudden attack had shocked and decimated Henry Binder. He would have been powerless to defend himself had he even thought to do so.

Hagerman's rage and frustration spewed out, uncontrolled, through his fists and feet. His massive, hairy, unclean hands smashed like sledges, bruising, tearing tissue, pounding Binder's unbelieving face and head, rattling his ledger brain in his unprotected skull.

Corporal Smith scurried to the phone to call the MPs even before Sergeant Binder hit the floor.

At the end of the beating, Hagerman was as subdued as the silent Binder. He retreated to a corner and sat on the floor with his back to the wall. He waited without word or thought for the inevitable military police. He offered no resistance when they roughly manacled his hands behind his back. He offered no information to the few, brief questions they asked. Before they led him away, he watched, unfeeling, as the medics carried out Binder on a stretcher. *Who was that fool?*

The general court-martial was short, uncomplicated and routine. Corporal Smith testified to the beating. Sergeant Binder was wheeled into the proceedings. His head jerked back and his eyes rolled with panic when Hagerman, in striped prison fatigues, came into his view. Binder shook uncontrollably and turned his face away. He held his trembling hand over his eyes when either the prosecution or defense council questioned him. His responses were vague and disconnected, interrupted by irrelevant rambling about Mrs. Binder, about Junior, about other times.

Richard Allen Anderson

~

Unable to serve, Henry Binder's military career ended with a medical discharge. Eventually, his scars became less violent, his bones and bruises healed, but his mind would not return. He disappeared into the streets of the homeless. He merged with other gray men and women without purpose or direction. The local cops sometimes returned his silent salute or sometimes prodded or smacked him lightly with their nightsticks, like a harmless stray dog.

Sometimes, late at night, the horror of his beating would replay in his mind as he huddled under a blanket or the cardboard shelter of a makeshift sleeping space, quietly whimpering.

Sometimes the shadow of a thought formed in the recess of his fractured mind . . . *What? Who? Why?*

~

Private Hagerman's sentence for assaulting a superior during a declared war included hard labor for three years plus jail time for the balance of his enlistment. Dishonorable discharge would eventually follow his term in maximum security.

Hagerman, the model prisoner, performed the hard and senseless prison labor willingly, almost eagerly breaking rock, shoveling earth, lifting, moving, sweating, aching. He spent his few leisure hours shining his boots and brass, straightening his bunk, and sitting erect on the backless stool in his small, barren cell.

His deep, black eyes stared ahead benignly, reflecting the inane vacuity of his prolonged incarceration. They no longer mourned, nor challenged, nor scowled. The Bison had been tamed. Sergeant Binder would have been so proud of him.

Richard Allen Anderson

14 April 1865

Miss Laura Keene is simply the most delightful thing—don't you agree?

Madam, I do agree, indeed! And Mr. Taylor's humorous script surely displays his wonderful English wit.

The gossip from New York and Boston has been exuberant, but still I never dreamed Our American Cousin would be so pleasurable a play.

My mind too has been captured for the time. . .not dwelling on our pressing matters.

Yes, I am happy for you. And I am so pleased that Major Rathbone and Clara Harris could join us for this occasion when General and Mrs. Grant were called away. They are so happy in their betrothal.

It is a pleasure to have their company, Mrs. Lincoln. But I am happy they decided to stretch their legs with a short walk before the intermission ends. It gives us these few unencumbered moments to chat—we get little enough time for that.

Our moments will never be unencumbered until this dreadful war concludes. I dream often of our future, away from wars and politics. Alone. At peace.

You must dream for us both then, Mary. I am consumed by the present. I continue to work with all my might and determination to bring this bloody conflict to a final conclusion. Still, your enjoyment of this performance has cheered me even beyond the optimistic war news. The dark veil of your depression has been pulled aside tonight. Here, put your hand in mine.

It's true. It is a rare moment that the ghost of our young son, Willie, does not haunt me. And now fears of

Robert's danger have come to haunt me as well. Why did you let him go to war?

You must not fear and fret for Robert, my dear Mary. He is not a child as Willie was, but a full-grown man of 22 years—safe on the staff of General Grant and even now in Washington. I pledge he will never compound your grief.

How can you make such a pledge? You could have prevented him from enlisting with the Union. Why did you let him go?

It was his choice, not mine. Not yours. Not ours.

You could have paid another to take his place. Thousands of the newly conscripted men have done so.

What then of honor, Mary? How could Robert learn of honor sending another to the war in his place?

Honor be damned!

Come dearest, you know he must not . . . cannot shirk. There are greater dangers to a young man than a rebel bullet.

But surely this horror must end soon. It has been days since Lee surrendered at Appomattox. Where will the war go now?

The wearied armies of North and South are both ready to lay down their arms. Our Union forces will prevail, of course. When they do so, a peace must be negotiated. Some will want to punish our southern brothers.

Yes, even some in your cabinet.

I cannot tolerate such thoughts and actions. We must ensure with the peace that our re-founded union will endure and gain new strength. We must turn our dedication to binding up the nation's wounds, caring for the battered veterans and for their widows and for their orphans. We must not have paid this dreadful toll for naught.

Your compassion will not be commonplace, Abraham, or shared by your political foes.

Your perceptions are always true, my dear. Even my generals have questioned how to treat the defeated Southern Armies. 'If I were in your place,' I told them, 'I'd let 'em up easy. Let 'em up easy.' There's been suffering enough.

Your hand feels deathly cold, Mr. Lincoln. Are you quite well?

Indeed I am, Mrs. Lincoln.

Secretary Stanton told me of your premonition of death today.

A foolish thing. It vanished as quickly as it came. Look here, the Major and Miss Harris have returned, and just in time to take their seats—the curtain has opened and the lights are down.

Is there someone else? Who entered our box just now? My God, he has shot the president! Call for the lights! Catch hold of him, Major! Look now, he's leapt upon the stage. Oh, my poor husband!

Sic semper tyrannis! Sic semper tyrannis! Sic semper tyrannis!

Richard Allen Anderson

An Interview with General James Longstreet

The Atlanta Constitution, March 16, 1890

This day, the Ides of March in the year 1890, is bleak and dismal in the hills of north Georgia. Since early morning, a light, cold rain has dampened the streets of Gainesville along with the spirits of its residents. It is a fitting day to visit this gravesite on the knoll at Alta Vista Cemetery, unmarked except for the Stars and Stripes hanging wet and forlorn from a short wooden staff at its head. Here, since January, lies Maria Louisa Longstreet, beloved deceased wife of General James Longstreet.

The view from this place is extensive. Tall trees off on the flats, reach to brush the morbid sky with limbs tinged in red and pale green, offering a subtle promise of coming spring.

This morning, in the city below, I interviewed the General, my former commander in the Army of Northern Virginia, where he was known as Old Pete to his troops. In his suite behind the tall, white columns of the luxurious Piedmont Hotel, General Longstreet's mood was somber, but he greeted me generously and answered my questions directly.

Atlanta Constitution: General, more than a quarter century has passed since I served under you as a young Sergeant in the ranks of First Corps. How are you today, Sir?

General Longstreet: My old war wounds are with me still. My right arm is paralyzed. My voice that once could be heard all along the lines is gone; I can scarcely speak above a whisper. My hearing is very much impaired. But enough of my injuries.

I am more distressed by other losses. Louise is gone from my life after more than forty years. My young bride was with me even while I was at war with the Mexicans and Indians. Even during the War of Northern Aggression. She bore me ten children, but five of my ten children have preceded me in death, some mere infants.

The same is true of many of those who served with me or against me in the war.

The General straightened here, almost at attention, fixed me with his dark eyes, his voice strained and barely audible when he continued.

I am almost 70. I am still vigorous, but at times, I wish the end would come. However, I have some misrepresentations of my battles that I wish to correct, so as to have my record straight before I die.

In spite of his voiced infirmities the General appears strong and vibrant, as able to lead and command as on that May day in 1864 when I witnessed his terrible wounding, shot through the throat and shoulder by a minie' ball—a victim of friendly fire at the Battle of the Wilderness.

His dark hair has turned startling white, and mutton-chop side-whiskers have replaced his massive beard. The fire behind his dark eyes alternately smolders and flares as he remembers and speaks.

Constitution.: At the Wilderness, I personally witnessed your leadership, your bravery, your dedication and your loyalty, General. Your Corps would have followed you anywhere. How will you rebut those who have attacked your military record and would detract from your achievements?

Longstreet.: I have started to write my memoirs again. Mr. Joel Chandler and Mr. Grady of your newspaper have kindly advised and assisted me. I base my writing on recorded fact, but I lost everything of that regard last year when fire destroyed our fine home and all its contents. All my records are gone, even my war souvenirs, my old uniforms, my sword.

Constitution.: General Jubal Early was the first to attack your record, your motives and your politics. Others, even Mr. Jefferson Davis, joined in his disparagement. How do you respond to them?

Longstreet.: I disagreed with President Davis on certain strategies of the war, but I will not speak against him, now he's gone. Jubal Early has attacked my performance at Gettysburg and stated that I cost the battle for insubordination and tardiness. Jubal Early is untruthful and incorrect. History will bear witness to my competence, my correctness.

The General's words came in a hoarse whisper tinged with both anger and regret. His left hand trembled as he poured two glasses of whiskey and silently offered one to me. He downed half his drink and continued, somewhat calmed.

Longstreet.: This right hand is of no use since the Wilderness. I have trained my left to take its place in most things, even writing. My memory has hardly faded on many points of history, and I will never forget a single detail of the first three days of July 1863.

Directly put, my dear, dead friend, General Robert E. Lee, was wrong at Gettysburg. George Pickett blamed him for the slaughter of his division until his dying day. He did not blame me, his immediate commander. He knew how I had advised for a flanking movement and against Lee's frontal attack tactics.

Early's generalling never was first rate. Gettysburg was no exception. Ewell and Early could have finished it that first day, but they hung back when the Federals retreated. Ewell and Early did not pursue, and that allowed the Federals to dig in and reinforce overnight. After that first night it was too late.

On July 2nd Ewell's delayed attack was of no assistance while my First Corp occupied the orchard and the wheat field and the Devil's Den.

On the last day, General Lee declined my strong suggestion for a flank attack, and we ordered Pickett's men forward into the center of the Federal defensive line. I could not speak but only nod my assent to Pickett for a frontal assault on Cemetery Ridge. We lost 20,000 good Confederate sons and husbands in that wheat field—mostly Pickett's, some of Hill's too. Most of the field officers were killed or wounded. The effort was nobly made but failed from the blows that could not be fended.

Pain distorted the General's face. He lowered his head, and I scarcely heard him as he strained to utter these last words: I loved the man! But he was wrong at Gettysburg.

General Longstreet finished his whiskey with one long draught and leaned back heavily in his large leather chair. His account had the ring of truth to it. Lee had called him his old warhorse, before and after Gettysburg. It was Jackson and Longstreet that Lee summoned as his first advisors on military matters, not Ewell or Early.

~

I had much more to ask about the General's life after Appomattox, about his Radical Republican politics in New Orleans, about compliance with Reconstruction, about his plans to rebuild his Georgia home. Those questions must await any future invitation to return to Gainesville for continued discussion. This interview ended when his young daughter burst into the room we had occupied alone until then.

Louise wept openly, grieving for her mother. "Papa . . . Papa . . . Papa," was all the girl could utter between convulsive sobs. The General held her to his chest with his strong, left arm and whispered words of consolation and commiseration until she became quiet. I heard her say finally, "I'm sorry Papa, but I miss her every minute."

The General's voice was gentle but determined when he said simply, "Lulu, we must bear our grief, and bravely, as your mama bore her suffering. Tomorrow the sun will shine, and we will ride with Fitz at the farm."

Louise smiled and softly kissed the General's cheek.

The General led me out through the anteroom in which hung the flag of our country with all 38 stars beside a torn Confederate infantry battle flag. Before we bade farewell to one another he whispered very quietly, almost to himself, "Why do men fight who were born to be brothers? This country was born the United States of America. It has been baptized in the blood of its own good citizens in that same name. Now let us let it be."

Historical Notes:

After the war, President Andrew Johnson refused to pardon Longstreet, stating, "There are three persons of the South who can never receive amnesty, Mr. Davis, General Lee and yourself. You have given the Union cause too much trouble."

The U.S. Congress restored his citizenship in 1868.

James Longstreet was one of few Civil War generals to live into the 20th century. After serving the Confederate States of America faithfully during the War Between the States, he served local, state and federal governments in various capacities including the posts of Ambassador to the Ottoman Empire and U.S. Commissioner of Railroads.

Longstreet married a second time in 1897 at age 76. His bride, Helen Dortch, was 34. Afflicted with severe rheumatism and cancer of the eye, he died of pneumonia six days before his 83rd birthday. He lies at rest in Alta Vista Cemetery in Gainesville, Georgia, near Louise and several of his children and grandchildren.

Bibliographical Notes:

Much of this fabricated interview draws on information from two primary references:
Lee's Tarnished Lieutenant by William Garrett Piston
The Killer Angels by Michael Shaara.
It also incorporates quotations in Longstreet's own words found at several internet web sites.

I recently rediscovered this piece of fiction I wrote in 2001 or 2002, long before I or anyone else owned a smartphone. I acquired my first iPhone for the singular purpose of using a dictation app to communicate with my deaf wife. I speak; the app prints my words on the display for her to read—at times, with hilarious or damnably frustrating results. Voice recognition has improved since then. A number of apps, including Google and Webster's Dictionary rarely misunderstand my gruff inquiries anymore.

Now that I use my iPhone to tell me what the weather is like in my back yard, to surf the internet, for texting, as a world atlas, a notebook, an encyclopedia, a stopwatch, a GPS, an emergency light, a HD digital camera, untold other uses including occasional phone calls, I am amazed at how prescient my vision for this story was. Apple now sells the tenth generation iPhone. The past six generations have embedded Siri, a female genie that lives in the phone and responds with her gentle voice to your every wish and command. I think they should have called her Maggie.

ALBERT AND MAGGIE TAKE THE PLUNGE

Albert had resisted entering the world of computers through the rise and fall of Microsoft, through the final demise of high-tech manufacturing and marketing giants Dell, IBM and Intel and well into the brave new world of do-all computing controlled by Ultimate Electronics Corporation.

UEC or "You-We Corp" as their ads proclaimed, had gained virtually immediate technical and marketing dominance with Maggie, displacing personal organizers, personal entertainment devices, personal computers, cellular telephones, digital cameras and assorted other business electronics and game gizmos.

Maggie was the brightest star in the cyber universe. Her diminutive heart was UEC's MAGPIE (Miniature Advanced Gigabyte Positive Ion Elucidator) universal coprocessor. The SUCCESS operating system (Simple Unified Computing, Communications, and Entertainment System Syntax) was the hand-held device's brain.

In short, Maggie did it all.

Albert inspected the contents of the small package from You-We Corp. Maggie was an appealing little thing, soft and warm in his hand, though still without life. He inserted the single power cell into Maggie's power port and watched the color CCD dawn into pale luminescence.

A seductive female voice drifted from the audio port. "I am Maggie, your personal servant. Please, tell me *your* name."

Startled by the inquiry, he stumbled, "Al. . .Al. . .Albert!"

"Hello Al, Al, Albert," the soft voice continued, "is that your full name?"

"Well, no," he said, "my full name is Albert Schleissweiger." He detected a faint note of irritation when Maggie spoke again.

"Please speak carefully and confirm your full name now."

"It's Albert. . . Albert Schleissweiger."

"Okay then Albert Albert Slicefinger, let's get started with the calibrations."

"Wait! It's not Albert Albert, it's just Albert, and it's not Slicefinger. It's Schleissweiger."

There was a long pause while Maggie's display flickered like heat lightning and flashed *MODE CHANGE FROM INTELLIGENT USER TO REMEDIAL.* Finally, she spoke again, but without the warm, inviting intonations Albert had heard earlier. "Okay Just Albert Slicewhiner. Is it permitted for me to call you Just?"

Albert opened his mouth to protest, stopped and quietly nodded his head in compliance. In a few moments, Maggie spoke again, "I know you have me in your hand, Just. Please respond now."

Albert swallowed hard. "Okay, fine. Just is just fine. But I'm not a Whiner, I'm a Weiger—Schleissweiger."

Maggie's voice rasped impatiently and her display throbbed, flashing alternately red and amber. "It appears I need to start your calibration before we can proceed. I'll call you Justfine for now."

Calibrate me? Albert funed, *this blinking box is going to calibrate me!*

"This is quite simple, Justfine, I hope you can handle it without difficulty or stress."

"Shoot!" said Albert, and the word conjured new, evil thoughts in his mind.

"I will say a word. You will repeat the word. Understood, Justfine?" Maggie was all business now.

"I understand."

"Please answer 'yes' or 'no'."

"Yes, damn it!"

"I take that to be 'yes'; 'damit' is not in my vocabulary."

Albert's hand commenced to tremble.

Maggie said, "There is instability in the hand-held position. It is permissible to place me gently on a firm and stable surface, Justfine."

Albert complied, standing Maggie upright on his desk in order to easily view her display that faded now to a pale blue indicating electronic equanimity.

"Thank you" said Maggie. "Now I will speak a word and you will repeat the word exactly. This is necessary for me to understand you. Ready?" She sounded a bit more cheerful now.

"Let's get it over with!" Albert did not try to hide his frustration.

The display acquired a tinge of yellow.

"Justfine," Maggie groaned, "answer 'yes' or 'no'."

"Yes," he replied aloud, and under his breath added, "damn it."

"Repeat the word 'albatross'."

Albert complied.

"Good. Now repeat the word 'Birmingham'."

He did, and his calibration proceeded through three alphabetic word lists with only three misses.

Finally, forty minutes after they started, Maggie prompted, "Your final word, Justfine. Repeat the word Zeitgeist."

Albert spit it out. "Zeitgeist, what the hell does that mean?"

"Please be patient, Justfine. You may open my dictionary and all communication functions after you have successfully recorded your password. But I think we both deserve a short break now; my micro-circuits are very warm. You may awaken me after five minutes by saying 'This is Justfine'. Understood?"

"Yes."

"Try it."

"This is Justfine."

"Excellent, Justfine. Goodbye." Maggie's display went dark.

Albert drummed his fingers on the desk, stood to stretch and glanced at his watch. He did ten pushups and checked his watch again. He felt humiliated, like a young schoolboy called to the principal's office then left to stew on the bench. He simmered until his patience slowly boiled away. He shouted, "This is Justfine!"

Maggie blinked awake immediately. "Hello, Justfine. Now we need to confirm your surname to use as your password. Please speak your name clearly."

"Schleissweiger."

"Slicewhiner," Maggie repeated.

"Schleissweiger!"

Maggie's display flashed *CORRUPT PCF* in red letters. Maggie said, "Your PCF has been corrupted, Justfine. We will recalibrate now."

Albert screeched, "PCF! PCF? What do you mean corrupted PCF?"

"That is your Pronunciation Calibration File."

Maggie's voice was deadly calm, but her display twitched in variegated shades of purple. "Estimated time for recalibration is 60 minutes." A digital clock appeared in Maggie's CCD, ready for the countdown. "Now I will speak a word and you will repeat the word exactly. This is necessary for me to understand you. Ready?"

"Ready, you oversexed radio—I'll show you ready!" Albert grasped Maggie tightly in his fist and shook her over his head.

Maggie's display flashed *ALARM MODE*. "Put me down, Justfine. Calm yourself. Where are you going? What-what are you doing?"

Her Surreptitious Lens emerged surreptitiously, and she recorded the horrifying scene in a series of digital photos stored deep in her mega-memory chips—Albert's sweaty countenance, teeth clenched in menacing grimace, the top of Albert's head, Albert's straining fingertips, and suddenly the gleaming white, vitreous sarcophagus.

Albert Justfine Slicefinger Schleissweiger walked deliberately to the bathroom and plunged Maggie into the cold, clear water of the commode. Maggie sparked once, then vibrated erratically in his hand. Her display scrolled one final message. *SCHLEISSWEIGER HAS COMMITTED FATAL ERROR! RETURN MAG . . . GIE . . . TO UEC . . . FOR SER . . . VICE!*

Albert released the trembling little box, reached up with his wet hand and flushed.

This story, with few modifications, was published in 2012 in West Georgia Living Magazine.

Shadows at Dawn

Have you ever wondered when, how and by whom in the course of humanity's evolution, the first word was spoken? If you have, as I have, you are not alone!

Theories on the origin of speech abound, but there are no clear answers on the subject, nor will there likely ever be. At one time (1866) the Linguistic Society of Paris banned debate on the subject at its meetings as being not only too contentious but totally futile. Most experts now agree that, interesting as these theories are, we do not and probably cannot come up with a definitive, meritorious answer.

So why think about it? Why commit effort, manpower and brainpower to the issue?

Speech and language ability are, among other traits like bipedalism, what distinguish humankind from all the other animals. Yes, other animals communicate with vocal utterances, though none by quite the same mechanism as humans use. Whales emit sonic squeals or songs that carry long distances in the ocean and communicate with other whales. Elephants on land communicate through low-frequency, inaudible (to humans) rumbles. The varied, cheery chirps of birds have been interpreted to have specific meanings to other birds. But none of these comes remotely close to human speech and language capabilities.

Early humans could not talk. While the history of humankind reaches back two million years or more, it is likely that extinct earlier forms of the species, Homo habilis and Homo erectus, advanced as they were over co-existing ape-forms, could not offer more than grunts and squeals, imitative sounds and signs as a means of communication. Anatomical evolution of speech organs, e.g. the larynx, mouth, throat and head, were prerequisite. Evolution of the brain seems certainly to have been prerequisite also, along with cultural or societal changes as the population grew, aggregated and dispersed across the planet.

The history of speech and of Homo sapiens may be one and the same. The ability to speak depended on the evolution of the physically and mentally advanced human species; the survival and advancement of the species depended on its ability to pass on detailed instructions, coordinate cooperative efforts, and to articulate abstract ideas. The rise of Homo sapiens began fewer than 200,000 years ago. Our ascendency to the premier species on earth was complete by 50,000 years ago.

But what of that first word? At some instant in time, with the evolutionary prerequisites in place, an individual must have synthesized a word that represented a thought, a concept, something beyond the grunts and yelps of warning or fear or joy.

Words are verbal icons. They are noises (or marks on stone or paper) that represent something either real or imaginary. Some say that language was invented to enable humans to lie, to represent as a sound an abstract or unreal idea. We can probably be confident that the perpetrator of that first word did not sit down, staring absently into the embers of a dying fire and think, "Today, I will invent language!" He or she probably did not consciously think at all, yet an all-important thought process occurred, an electro-chemical process in the brain that had not occurred before, but would be repeated in all surviving generations.

My prose poem, "Shadows at Dawn," was first published in 2016 in my second collection of poems, *Potholes in Memory Lane.*

Shadows at Dawn

Homo X, with dreadful reverence,
draws up his muscled arms
points ahead toward the east
extending long and bristled fingers
toward the magical aurora
and as the golden rim appears
raises voice to sustain a sound
o o o o o o o o   o
a simple sound
suffuse with complex, primitive emotion:
awe and gratitude, fear and pleasure.

The small band of huddled beings
emerging from the cavern's mouth
sends forth a joyful, manic chorus
across the grassy plain
into the distant shadowed forest—
O O O O O O O O O O . . .

They stand erect and elevate their arms
join their fingers above their dimly lighted faces.
Another day to hunt and forage.
Another day to risk at living.

Richard Allen Anderson

Homo X leaps upon a high flat rock
his place of honor, his platform to survey
and lead the morning mystic ritual.
The first bright rays surmount the trees, illuminate
his fearsome face, his massive chest, his extended limbs.

An unforetold, unwanted force stirs within his brain,
an awareness of a furtive presence deep within.
His ferocious eyes dart and race,
absorb the full extent of his own being.
His strong hands press against the turmoil in his skull.
A sound stirs unsummoned within his throat—
Aaah Aaah

The sound persists within him, seeking to escape
forcing his heavy lips apart
then bursts forth to startle and bewilder
the others and himself. Ah!
And then another even stranger sound. Ya!

A simian smile distorts his face.
With lips parted and drawn back
ahya he whispers, ahya, then shouts
Ahya. Ahya. Ahya!

He whirls about to face the fearful group.
Sunlight exaggerates the shadow of his broad shoulders
and makes serpents of his upraised arms upon the ground.

He points a finger at his chest
and now forcefully, willfully, articulates
the syllables of self-image—Ahya!
With wonder in his newfound power—Ahya. Ahya.
Concept burgeons into Comprehension.

He jumps with simple joy, high in the still air,
returns to his haunches, springs high again, again.
He beholds the sunlit, shadowed brows
of his gathered species-homo family.

They stare agape in fearful apprehension.

Homo X descends
from his altar of enlightenment
pervaded now with understanding
a new connection fused, a virgin neuron pathway
somewhere within his primal brain.

He grasps the hand of each fellow being
to place it against its own naked breast and,
eyes ablaze, speaks the magic syllables—

Ahya.

First one,
then two or three,
not comprehending
but submissively compliant
attempt the sound
Aah. Aah. Ahya. Ahya.

The embryonic thought ascends
displacing shadows of ignorance.
They slap their arms, their chests,
their now wide-eyed faces
acknowledging with ape-like grins
their dawning understanding
their linking of thought and sound.

A word is born
one simple utterance:

Within it
the seeds of human perception
communication, language, intelligence.

Within it
the plays and poetry
of Sophocles, Shakespeare, Ibsen.

Within it
the analects of Confucius
the Magna Carta,
the Declaration of Independence
the Communist Manifesto.

Within it
an infinity of unimagined worlds.

As to the Title

This book is a collection of short fiction.

All fiction is a lie intended to reveal the truth.

Taradiddle is a lie, a minor falsehood, a bit of pretentious nonsense.

And cookie crumbs are those small, savory bits of sweetness and pleasure too good to merely sweep away, random, scattered remnants.

I hope you find my lies, the stories gathered into this book, as satisfying as those last crumbs of your favorite cookie.

Richard Allen Anderson
September 2019

Richard Allen Anderson

Acknowledgements

I wish to recognize and thank the members of the Carrollton Writers Guild, "Just Prose" group for listening to many of the stories in this collection and for offering their insightful critiques and constant encouragement.
Elyse Wheeler, Frank Allen Rogers and Stephani Baldi of that group were especially helpful with the final editing.
John Bell of Vabella Publishing provided invaluable and essential assistance in bringing the book into print.